I0771283

# WILL SHAKESPEARE

## and the Ships of Solomon.

### CHRISTOPHER GREY.

*Basilicus Press*
*Los Angeles*

For my loving and wicked-awesome wife. Without you I may be able to write books, but they'd be terrible.

And for my son. At 6 I know you'd prefer this book feature dinosaurs and Lego guys, but I aspire to write fiction that you will one day love.

Montreal, Quebec
September 6, 1947.

# ONE

Sir William Shakespeare lit a cigarette to pass the time. Even through the fog he could make out the silhouettes of the surrounding landmarks in Old Montreal. On this particular overcast day, the city was more akin to London than Paris, from which many locals declared their heritage. Will spent a great deal of time in both cities and could personally attest to the ambiance of each. No matter what the charcoal skyline of this city presented or feigned, it was no doubt as cold as London. His wool overcoat did little to help, and the gray fedora on top of his well-combed black hair only stopped the moisture from disrupting the hair treatment.

Blue eyes scanned the skyline. It was the most interesting place to look. Cowering fog oppressed the Canadian cityscape with little regard for daylight. Traffic down St. Catherine's was all but extinct. Every twenty minutes or so a distant hum of a car would be complemented by fading headlights as they turned from Union or University, submitting to the thick moisture by employing useless headlights. It was infrequent enough that he could spend a great deal of time examining them as they passed, refracting in dismal displays of frigidity. Pontiacs ... Chevys ... gray ... beige ... black... . Nothing to cause concern.

The humidity was high enough to turn the city into a veritable swimming pool; such was not uncommon for this time of year. Only the day prior a storm passed through, throwing down sheets of incessant rain, taking away fallen leaves and other autumn debris into the confluence of the Saint Lawrence and Ottawa Rivers. A frigid day coming out of an even more brisk night cost many Montrealers a pleasant morning. In just a short time, snow would mark the landscape and herald a long winter ahead.

Brown bristles of deleafed deciduous trees from the largest green space in the city combed over the gentle slope of Mount Royal, which stretched, devoid of people, into the throngs of McGill University. A forest of meager but still prominent buildings decorated the campus and lowland shores on the east end of the island, humbly marking Montreal's downtown area. Not quite in the vicinity of Old Montreal, but close enough to see the Gothic fingers of aged colonial skyscrapers and churches, lay one of the more prized structures in the well-populated *Ville-Marie* borough. The Christ Church Cathedral, promenading an entire city block, catapulted its own religious testament toward the already aged and humbling skyline. Buried next to McGill's nineteenth-century manicured campus and amid one of the larger commercial districts of the borough, it was a more permanent marker on the skyline.

Beneath the skyline and at the enclave of the cathedral, Will watched for any unusual activity. Pedestrians were just as scarce as cars, if not more so. No one in their right mind would be walking down St. Catherine's on this morning. Not unless they were a McGill student or hopelessly lost. *It wasn't St. Catherine's*, Will corrected himself. The locals called it *Rue Ste-Catherine O*. The French pride here took some getting used to, and even after two years he was nowhere near tolerant enough. Living in Montreal did affect his French, however, and on a good day he could very easily get around using the language. He already had a base from his years in Vietnam, but the dialect was very different. His French-Canadian accent was strange enough that most people didn't even guess he was American, much less a Connecticut native.

The delicate lights inside Christ Church Cathedral danced from behind stained glass. It was likely quite a lot warmer in there, and as much as he'd like to go in, he couldn't. His job was to make sure no one went inside who wasn't authorized by the Order. With the complete lack of passersby, the job was far easier than he'd thought it would be.

The regular churchgoers and staff weren't a problem, as Will had arranged to have the facility completely vacated three days before. The Order had high contacts within the Anglican Church, and it really only took verification of who they were to keep the facility clear. The staff closed the doors to the public, citing plumbing problems, and ensured that the congregation was well aware of the issue. That wouldn't disrupt normal services, as everyone would be out by evening, allowing the clergy to prepare for the next day's sermon.

It was three-thirty the last time he checked his watch, and that was recent enough that he didn't bother to check again. Looking at his watch too many times made the time pass slower. They'd been in there for four hours—a very long time to watch nothing, although Will was accustomed to this sort of work. During the secret war of the mid-1930s, he'd spent countless hours in the dark streets of Havana watching walls rot. The jungles of Vietnam were no different. Even his work on the Allied fronts of the war kept him at watch more than once. The secret was simple: watch the horizon and focus on points only when there was movement.

Very important men were inside the church at the moment discussing things Will had no earthly idea about. The last time the commanders were all in the same room was the dawn of the war. If the threat of Nazi Germany was the one thing that brought these old men together, it horrified Will to know what had gathered them here on this day.

The 1939 meeting was a much different time, even though it was less than ten years prior. He was still a knight, but the work in 1938 put him on the path to promotion, earning him the prestigious title of turcopolier. His work in Havana with Lucky Luciano and other Mafioso leaders secured private interest in Cuba from rising communist influence. Suddenly wrenched from the secret affairs of the Latin world, Will was dropped directly into the middle of Europe while a madman marched across the landscape. Will wasn't the only one dispatched. In fact, the crew present in Montreal that day was the very same one that had kept each other alive in the European war. If it wasn't world war these men were meeting about, Will didn't really want to know what it was.

The grounds were clean. He and Sam Adams had just completed

a fourth sweep. There were six other sergeants patrolling the area. No one was getting through. He stayed with Sam, his prodigy, at the front. There were two men on either side of the cathedral, and two patrolling the perimeter. Will had asked for more knights--or even sergeants, but the commanders weren't able to bring them back to Montreal soon enough. Many were still supporting the security of Berlin's occupation, and after recent outbursts in Vietnam against the French, a dozen were placed back there.

His curiosity was piqued, but any guesses on his part would only be speculation. Knowing the meeting took place under the direst of necessities, he also knew that the Order was in great danger. Having all members of the entire leadership in one place was rarely practiced, and for good reason. A secret society needed safeguards in place to ensure the knowledge of its members was not lost. Whatever brought them all to Montreal was no concern to Will—he was a soldier. He didn't need to know the politics behind his organization. He followed orders as he always did.

Keeping trained eyes on the distant Montreal background, he pondered the location. Out of all the world's cities in which the Order operated, their base of operations was this somewhat small city in Canada. Knowing the full history of the Order meant it was no mystery. In fact, the city of Montreal was created on the Order's influence as a sort of Utopian society. Fighting the impulse to use the word *Utopian*, he reminded himself that the city more appropriately represented the concepts described in Francis Bacon's novel *New Atlantis*. Montreal was the center of a New Scotland with high liberal ideals. These concepts were still inbred in the society, it seemed. Just three years prior, there had been great national conflict when the mayor protested conscription for the war. Ottawa put the mayor in prison, and the conscription was enforced.

Will was somewhat dismissive about Canada. He didn't particularly care for the climate and was accustomed to slightly more exciting locations. Used to being in the center of it all, adjusting to the slow-paced northern life wasn't without its challenges. No longer concerned for his life whenever he stepped outside his house, and working a somewhat regular job with the Order training sergeants, the days of working the field were sorely missed. He'd also been stuck as a trainer for long enough that he hadn't managed to make it to his home town, Hartford, since the war. A ping of guilt crossed his consciousness as he recalled Hartford. It had been too long.

Will had been promoted to turcopolier during the war, a fantastic honor and one awarded to only three dozen people in the entire world. He was in command of the sergeants of the *Pauperes Commilitones Christi Templique Salomonici* and had access to some of the most powerful secrets in human history. Part of becoming a knight in the first place, however, was erasing his old identity. He was now immersed in an ancient tradition and as such operated above any nation or society on the planet. He could no longer be a normal citizen. He took a vow of poverty and of chastity. His old life was over, and a new, secret one had begun. One in service of God and of man. The knighthood faked his death in the war and sent reports home to his mother and sister that he'd died honorably in combat in Germany. He would never contact his family again.

Those were distant and painful thoughts to have on this morning, and so he sidetracked himself by checking the position of his crew. Glancing back, he made sure Adams was still in position. Nothing had changed. As turcopolier, however, security was on his shoulders. He couldn't allow any of the sergeants to lose focus. The commanders had tightened security for a reason. His reevaluation of the crew brought his attention to another oncoming car.

This one was different from the others. Immediately Will knew it wasn't a civilian. The pace was too slow as it crawled forward deliberately. The driver was making no mistakes, watching for every conceivable detail. Even in fog, civilians tend to move forward with a flare of recklessness. Content to crouch behind their steering wheels and squint into the white nothingness, they think that by squinting they'll see something before it becomes a problem. A military person, however, will simply travel more slowly, having built the fog into the mission as a component.

The car stopped precisely in front of the cathedral, close enough that Will could spot the signature maple-leaf Canadian flags attached to the hood—far too showy for his tastes. He had been expecting this car. Ottawa was personally escorting a civilian for the leadership to interview. That's all he knew. Given the security concerns, he was appalled they'd arrived in diplomatic style. Anyone with half a brain would know something important was happening at the cathedral today. Their low profile was effectively blown.

His face darkened as he watched a man step out of the backseat in a pressed navy-blue suit and yellow tie, black overcoat, and fedora. A public servant, not a spook. *Why were they being so careless?*

The politician opened the back door and helped out another passenger. Will had taken the vows and he was a professional, but he did take an interest in the woman who stepped out. Short brown hair. Youthful face but with years behind her brown eyes. She was sun-kissed yet dressed like a New Yorker. He allowed himself enough leeway to lose focus for only a second. Long enough to nod and offer an obligatory smile as they approached. But long enough to feel the stab of guilt that inevitably follows temptation.

"Miss Wilkinson, for you, my friend," the politician said.

Glancing back at Sam Adams, Will gave the unspoken order to hold his position while he escorted the guest. Adams, standing at ease, snapped into focus and put out his cigarette, now being the eyes of the operation. Shakespeare was free to greet the newcomers.

"Good afternoon, Miss Wilkinson, we appreciate your prompt arrival. You are free to go inside."

Will kept his smile, but it was only an act. He was being polite because she was a civilian, and possibly because she was pleasant to look at, but much more important issues were on his mind. *I am not a doorman.*

The woman smiled and hesitantly went into the cathedral, looking back at the politician as she did so. As soon as she was out of sight, Will's smile dissolved into severity. He broke through the politician's milk-toast expression with an unblinking and official stare.

"You took a public vehicle. Why?"

"I thought your guest should arrive in style," he said with a high tone in his voice, emoting a certain level of offense.

"Before you leave, remove those flags. Tell the driver to dump the car at the university."

Now the man was openly offended.

"Wait a minute, sir! Do you have any idea who I am? You are talking to ..."

"An elected official, yes I know. You are compromising our security."

"Just who do you think you are?" his voice was raised now.

"If you have to ask, you are not cleared to know. Leave the car at McGill's. Find another way back."

"This is ridiculous. I'm calling the office!"

Will looked back at Adams with another unspoken order. The sergeant immediately stepped forward and opened his coat. The sidearm was quite visible underneath.

This openly threatening gesture stunned the official into silence. Sputtering and glancing between both men with a reddened face, the Canadian did what he was told, removing the flags and crawling inside the vehicle. Will watched him go with no expression. He only hoped it would be enough. They could already be compromised.

He turned to Adams. "Walk the perimeter again. Make absolutely sure it's clean."

Adams nodded and went on his way.

Will reflected on this woman and how she'd arrived. There was no good reason a woman like that would be meeting with the grand master and the commanders. Slamming his mind back into focus, he finished his cigarette and took a good look around the premises. Moving down the steps of the church, he checked around the corner to see if any headlights were approaching.

It was a good thing he did because in the next moment he was forced to pull his gun.

# TWO

It had been a rather uncomfortable trip. Dorothy Wilkinson had left the blissful warm coasts of Bermuda fourteen hours prior on a commercial airliner, her first ever flight, and landed in Montreal. Greeted with nothing but cold and fog, she'd bundled up in the only coat she owned—a light cotton shawl—and her navy skirt, jacket, and the white blouse her father bought on her birthday. It was meant for a trip to Europe they'd planned in the winter. Until yesterday, she'd thought she wouldn't put it on until then.

Her father's flu had become progressively worse over the week, and by the time Friday had come around, he was confined to bed with nothing but broth in the evening and lots of fluids the rest of the day. Like every year, he caught the bug from the fall tourists as they clambered off their boats to see the sights of Bermuda. He insisted on going into town for fresh produce even during the busiest tourist seasons. There was nothing he loved more than fresh papaya. This time the cost was higher. The bug had progressed into pneumonia, and he was bedridden on doctor's orders.

She now had to represent the family on her father's business. This was not the first time she'd done this and, in fact, did it a great deal in Bermuda. This was the first time, however, that her father had sent her abroad in his place. Generally, her work was alongside her father in local banks or boardrooms. Sometimes they even met clients on passenger ships. Her father's business was rather extensive, and although he traveled frequently, she'd never gone with him.

Being limited to Bermuda, Dorothy Wilkinson had never been in a cathedral. Although she'd been raised Anglican, the churches in Bermuda were a far cry from the church in Montreal. It was difficult to believe that her denomination built such Gothic structures. It was absolutely breathtaking inside. She'd stepped in from the West Door and with interest passed the gold-tiled nave. As she pressed onward, she saw the High Altar blossom ahead like a stained-glassed waterfall, cascading elegance onto the floor and pews below. One would only know this was Anglican from the lack of crucifixes. A simple cross adorned either side of the altar. To the left was a decorative stone pulpit.

Instead of a reverend, there was a homely older man wearing a mismatched navy-blue and black suit. Thick glasses hung like lead on his bulbous face, and the last shreds of hair on his head were dissipated into white strands. The alleged congregation was full of men no younger than fifty. They all wore suits, ties, and curious lapel pins showing a red cross on a white shield. The chapel was quiet, but that soon ended with Dorothy's arrival.

"Ah, Miss Wilkinson, please come forward. I would like to introduce you to your father's investors. We are anxious to hear news of the property."

She hadn't expected this. A boardroom, perhaps in some nearby building. Or a bank. A banker's office, even. But a Gothic church? And why were these men seated as if listening to a sermon? All her father had told her was that these men had to know about the storm. They were so invested in knowing what was going on that they'd paid for her flight to Montreal. Flights were reserved for the elite, especially from Bermuda to Canada. These men must have been very serious about the investment and were very wealthy to demand her father's presence. After learning of his illness, they'd demanded a trusted proxy. There was no doubt this situation was dire.

Meeting in a church, however, was unsettling.

"Good afternoon, gentlemen. I'm sure you have heard of what we are up against."

The old man in the pulpit nodded. "Yes. You may not be aware, Miss Wilkinson, but we have a very important investment on your property. We fear that this storm may compromise it. We have been discussing our options this morning, and it is not exactly simple to relocate our investment. Your father said you have a survey?"

"Frankly, it isn't good ..." She didn't know what to call them. No one had mentioned anyone's name. The whole thing gave her a bad feeling. She trusted her father with her life and would never suspect that he was involved in something illegitimate, but she couldn't get past the secrecy of it all.

"I beg your pardon," she said, interrupting herself. Clearing her throat, she looked around her at the pews and then ahead toward the pulpit, feeling as if she were on trial. "I don't know your name ... or your organization."

A few chuckles sounded from around her, and the old man at the pulpit smiled. "No, I don't suppose that you do. We are a private organization that has several worldwide interests. You can call me 'Mr. Jackson.'"

This didn't help her comfort level in the least. Used to meeting with all casts of people, she'd never seen the likes of these men. They were all very official-looking, almost governmental, in fact. What was more unsettling was that they had property on their land in Bermuda. Although she very much wanted to know what it was, or at least the nature of it, the defensive comeback told her that it would remain a mystery. Resigning herself to the current state of things, she looked around once more and cleared her throat.

After numerous meetings with her father working with real estate tycoons, ship manufacturers, and marketing firms, such dismissal was rather common, especially when people were dealing with a woman. It was clear these old men didn't believe she had the credentials to know too much and that they would treat her only as a proxy. The truth was, her father had spent the last four years preparing her to take over the family business. In his eyes, she was a partner, not just a proxy. However, she supposed there was no point in making these men feel uncomfortable. Their business methods seemed odd enough that she didn't want to know much about their true nature or whether their organization was in any way unscrupulous. They were obviously strong investors, and the family needed these types of clients. It would be a harsh blow to her father to learn that they might be illegitimate in some way.

With hesitant resignation, she continued and stepped forward to hand Mr. Jackson a file folder she'd been poring over for the past couple of days. Included were various local weather reports, as well as some meteorological commentary they'd wired from the University of Miami. Her father had also commissioned a surveyor to create maps, analyze soil samples, and produce a diagnostic. She shuddered to think how much the report cost, and oddly she was not permitted to see the purchase orders. At first she thought it was only because her father had the flu and was anxious to get her on her way, but after meeting these men, she suspected he didn't want her to be too shocked at the cost. Hopefully, their bill to the investors would easily overcome the report cost.

"Here is the survey. It seems some of the northwest caverns are compromised. This survey suggests that if even a small storm hits, then the entire face of this hill will collapse and so will the caverns beneath it. I assume this is your property?"

She was quite familiar with the so-called "hill" the geologist had surveyed. Having grown up on the property, she knew almost every meter of it. Her sister would join her for spelunking in the Crystal Cave beneath their property and afterward would often go to this hill and watch the tide recede so they could crawl down the hillside and investigate the crabs and tropical fish trapped in the tide pools. She'd asked her father if this organization owned the cave, and he assured her they didn't. The only conclusion she could draw from that was that they were storing something in the caves.

This unsettled her. Whatever was being stored there was not only very valuable but also very secret. Those caves wound all throughout that part of Bermuda for kilometers. No one had successfully charted the whole area. Even her grandfather, who'd discovered the caves, hadn't seen half of them. He gave her grand tours of course, and there were some places he cautioned her against because they were dangerous. Even if she'd seen those places, she still wouldn't know the full extent of them. It was the perfect place to hide something very secret. There were very few reasons to go to those lengths to hide something.

Coupled with this odd meeting, she was growing quite suspicious of this organization, as well as some of the other important business deals her father had been leaving her out of. She was somewhat irked that she hadn't been made aware of these clients, and with their obvious wealth, they seemed to be good clients to know. Although it was *possible* her father was involved in some shady deals, it wasn't likely. He had a lot of character. But perhaps she only wished that to be true.

Mr. Jackson's face turned serious as he reviewed the photographs, maps, and charts. "It is Mr. Wilkinson's property," he said, "but it could indeed affect our property as well. Can you tell me about this storm?"

"It is a tropical storm out of Cape Verde. The University of Miami is unsure about where it is headed, but we are convinced it will become a hurricane. If it comes anywhere near Bermuda, then this part of the cave will be flooded from the swell. If you look at photograph B1, you will see the compromised soil. A very small storm could breach that, and it would be enough to allow the tide in, especially a swell of over two meters."

"Why has this never happened before?"

"Nature," Dorothy said, shrugging. "The earth erodes, Mr. Jackson. It just so happened that my father noticed this ditch where the soil collapsed. The damage was probably from last month's storm, but this has been thousands of years in the making."

"When?"

"It's impossible to say. If it continues to move as quickly as it is now, it could be there by the tenth."

"Six days," he whispered to himself.

"It could be as many as twelve days. Large storms tend to slow down as the seas cool around them. If it remains hot in the south, however, we can expect it to keep up its momentum. Miami doesn't think it will hit Bermuda directly. In fact, they are charting it for a direct hit in the Caribbean, but even that far away, the wind and the swell would be very impressive." She halted at the last statement, realizing it sounded unsympathetic. "I mean to say, of course, it is enough to do the deed."

That news wasn't any better. Mr. Jackson set the papers on the pulpit and ran stressed fingers across the bridge of his nose. There was a long silence, which caused Dorothy to glance up at the others. Sullen and distant, they watched Mr. Jackson carefully, as if he were going to create a miracle and save them all from this apparent devastation. He remained quiet. Removing his glasses, he looked at the congregation and heaved a sigh.

"Gentlemen, do you have any more questions for Miss Wilkinson?"

Dorothy wished her father hadn't gotten the flu. This was no place for her. She had no idea who these clients were or of their interest in her father's property. Opening the forum for questions would do no good because she'd revealed absolutely everything she knew. This was not her usual turf. Quite comfortable in Bermuda without American and Canadian accents, she felt like an alien inside these walls. Her confidence in front of these mysterious strangers was beginning to crumble, and much more of this would cause her to openly falter. She couldn't understand why her father simply hadn't asked them to come to Bermuda like he did all his other clients.

She looked up, hoping that no one would ask any questions. To her dismay, one man did. He was also older, like most of the gentlemen there. His gray hair was thinning, but he had a very strong and almost youthful face. He didn't look frail like Mr. Jackson; he resembled some of the British or U.S. military leaders she saw back home—broad shoulders, forceful gaze, and perfect posture.

Standing straight he said, "Good morning, Miss Wilkinson. On behalf of the others present, I thank you for coming out on such short notice. My name is s ..." He stopped on that consonant and looked up at Mr. Jackson as if he'd slipped. Then, after looking back to her, he said, "Mr. Franklin. Tell me, ma'am, how long does it take to get to Bermuda?"

There was a question she could answer.

"Fourteen hours."

"Eh ... by ship?"

"It is faster to go by plane, Mr. Franklin."

His harsh eyes faltered with a hint of frustration, but he recomposed himself.

"Yes, I know, but that may not be an option. How long by ship?"

"Two to three days, I suppose. It depends, of course, on the ship and its capabilities."

"Thank you, Miss Wilkinson."

He sat and whispered to a colleague next to him.

"Anything else?" Mr. Jackson asked the church. When no one responded he said, "Tell your father that we will be moving our investment before the storm hits, and as always, his discretion is appreciated."

Just then, there was the distinct sound of gunfire coming from outside.

# THREE

It was a somewhat unpleasant morning, with impending fog, bristling temperatures, and drenching humidity. *Rue Ste-Catherine O* was free of cars. Not even the pious walked along the sidewalks. Not a single young adult with a bag slung over a shoulder was anywhere in sight. As Will scanned the perimeter, he realized also that McGill's was not even two blocks away. It was unusual for a downtown area next to a college campus to be completely abandoned on a Saturday in the middle of term. It was only at that moment Will noticed this fact, and it seeped into his consciousness like a clamp. This was a main downtown thoroughfare, and although the street traffic would be light in mid-afternoon, it would not be empty. Not on a Saturday.

Years of field experience and training whispered several orders into his inner ear. Adrenaline sticking its toes into his bloodstream, Will's senses were exponentially heightened. Instinct alone brought his hand inside the wool jacket, where it fell upon the familiar form of his Smith & Wesson tucked underneath his arm in a hidden holster. He whipped his wrist outside his breast pocket and carefully eased the pistol into his hand. Stepping backward, his blue eyes looked up and down the street, though his head didn't move. One would have to be very close by to notice his search.

A rehearsed, casual gesture then followed. He tilted his gray fedora upward. This would cause anyone watching to think he was idly guarding, not actively searching. It also drew attention away from the weapon in his hand. Although it was pointed downward and his arm was relaxed, it would be all too easy to notice his heightened maneuvers. With another practiced casual move, Will walked back toward his post, dropping his shoulders, signaling that he'd done his job for that hour and was returning to his waiting position. In reality, he was examining the position of the other knights.

Adams was in place at the entrance, just about to head out on the sweep he'd been ordered to do. Bill Cody and John Paul Jones were ten paces over, keeping watch over the intersection of *Rue University* and *Rue Ste-Catherine O.* Oscar Wilde was on the other side of the church, strolling unknowingly with a cigarette hanging from his aging mouth. Adams was the first to notice Will's actions, and he immediately straightened his composure. It was, perhaps, too late.

Two black sedans swung around the corner of *Rue University*. Parking single file at the curb in front of the church, wheels burning to a stop. Will immediately darted under the awning of the church, Adams at his heels, but even as he went he knew they were in immense danger.

It was an ambush.

Will brought his pistol into formal grip, thankful he'd drawn it. His left arm braced his firing arm. He fell back behind the stone arches of the church façade, feeling Adams' presence behind him facing the other side of the arch. Raising the gun upward, he squinted through the moisture, hoping to glean their moves before opening fire. Though it wasn't likely, he had to be sure these people weren't civilians simply acting like reckless idiots.

The passenger-side doors fell open on the far side of the car. The drivers ducked down and out of sight, while two passengers in each car climbed out. Before taking shots, Will waited for the targets to give away their intentions. It wouldn't take long. They wore dark suits and hats, and through the windows he saw the unmistakable profile of Thompson submachine guns.

Adams saw them too; pushing backward the young sergeant eyed his mentor. There was no doubt what these men intended to do.

Will couldn't evaluate or even command his crew, and so he had to trust them. Drawing his second sidearm, usually only a backup, he stepped out from behind the Gothic arches.

When a firefight began, all those involved stepped into another world. Pumped up with a natural superhuman drug, they noticed every little detail and sound as if it were blaring through megaphones. It was the experienced ones, however, who could take the sensory tornado and harness it into an effective combat machine. Like dozens of times before, Will Shakespeare was on the wrong end of an invasive maneuver. Four men in secret uniforms unleashed a fury of bullets. Exploding shells rattled through the air and crashed through stone and dirt. In a stream of sparks, the impact deafened anyone nearby. Shakespeare used his heightened senses to note which way the stream was going.

Deciding it was safe enough to return fire, Will let loose a hail of bullets at the sedans. Squeezing the triggers of both guns as fast as his joints allowed, four discharges pounded the biceps of both arms before he saw the gunners backing away and taking shelter behind the opened doors of their cars. Next to him he heard Adams firing before returning to his haven under the arches, and distantly, from either side of the church, his other crew also let loose, apparently having found cover as well.

Their offense was short-lived. Now that the men had found cover and their bullets crashed through the windows or burrowed harmlessly into the insides of the cars, the menace would return with a more established and fierce round of gunfire. The opposition had semiautomatic weapons, which was a distinct advantage against his men and their comparably weak sidearms.

Strategies poured through Will's mind as he reloaded both weapons. He was prepared only for security, not a war. Shoving aside his curiosity as to the attackers' identity, he stuck strictly to military mode. Glancing up to see Adams reloading as well, he gestured with his head to give Adams a command. The signal was clear. They needed to get out from under the arches and establish a solid group with the others. This would be tricky under such heavy gunfire, but the only way they could get back at those Tommys was to create a massive frontal attack.

The technique had worked in Vietnam with the French. Shakespeare charged with an infantry company of only twenty men, but their consolidated numbers allowed them to burrow through the toughest part of the front, effectively collapsing the company's strength. Once established inside the company, the men spread outward and the nationalists retreated into the forest. It could work here too. They needed to charge the sedans as one unit from the side, minimizing the enemy's cover. It would only work with all of his men, and it left the church entrance uncomfortably vulnerable.

Several more rounds were exchanged. Two more gunmen stepped out from the backseats of the sedan and fell into advancing formation on the church. The monolithic figure of a bald man also appeared from one of the sedans. His black suit was impeccable, and he wore thick glasses over completely expressionless eyes. Stone cheeks and a firm nose suggested a very lengthy military background. This man was the one in charge. He didn't bother pulling a weapon but rather surveyed his strategy.

The rattling of the Tommys subsided. They were either reloading or repositioning. Either way the silence burned. Will peered out from the arches and saw the attackers cowered behind the cars, reloading. The Tommys were temporarily stalled. Now was the time. Adams and Will jumped out from the arches, firing repeatedly. The force of their attack caused the enemy to immediately take cover. The black-suited monolith even ducked behind the front of one of the cars. Crashing windowpanes and exploding steel rang through the fog as Will and Adams bounded around the bush-covered corner of the church. The slick grass consumed their sprint, and their polished shoes skidded into a flat spin behind the corner. Now safe from the Tommys, they kept low behind the corner as pieces of stone and plaster rained on top of them.

Will assessed the situation. Wilde was hit. His gray suit showed redness on its shoulder and down the arm. Despite the injury, he was reloading, preparing for another volley. Frightened brown eyes regained confidence at the sight of his two comrades. Bullets rained over them, and Will dragged Wilde backward to keep him out of the way.

As the older man continued to load his weapon, Will jerked back Wilde's suit jacket. The bullet had taken part of the shirt into the wound, and it clung tightly to the increasing pool. Brief analysis suggested the bullet had entered just below his collarbone. Far enough from the heart to not be deadly, it was, however, close enough to a major intersection of muscles to nearly paralyze his right arm. A right-handed soldier would have to fire with his left hand. The exit wound would also be larger. Wilde would lose a lot of blood from this wound. Without medical attention in the next two hours, he'd be falling into serious shock. Looking back up at Adams, Will raised his eyebrows to suggest that the diagnosis wasn't good. Adams took note of the gesture and then checked around the corner to assess their position.

"We have to take them head on," Will said to Wilde.

He grunted, finally finishing the loading procedure, and after trying to secure the pistol in his right hand, Will's fears were realized. Seizing in pain, Wilde dropped the pistol. Gray eyebrows fell into resignation, and he picked it up with his left hand.

"Can you run?" Will asked.

Weakened eyes peered upward at Will before moving past his shoulder to the rattling scene ahead. Taking a firmer grip on his pistol, Wilde nodded. He closed his eyes, quietly preparing, and then hoisted himself up with his good arm. Swaying and stumbling a little, he regained his balance by leaning on Adams. They all paused to see if he was stable, and based on his affirmative and determined expression, Will saw that he was.

"Adams, cover."

Will looked around the corner. Explosions and gunfire waned into short bursts. Four gunners were reloading, and two more had joined them. Their attention was caught by short blasts on the other side of the church. Cody and Jones were still actively engaging the enemy.

The attackers' guns would be loaded soon, and two of the men pivoted to find their target. In a matter of seconds, two Tommy guns would be ripped open on the other corner of the church.

Will held up a flat hand to signal that they should stay put. The two menaces would be reloaded and ready to fire within seconds.

That would allow enough time for the wounded to make it through to the arches, especially if the enemy's attention was diverted. He pointed to Wilde and then with a fist ran his arm up and down. This signaled that Wilde would make a break for it. He then pointed to himself and Adams, pointing his finger in the shape of a gun to signal that he and Adams would cover him. To launch the commands he simply pointed forward.

Holding two guns each, Will and Adams jumped out from cover and unloaded on the first sedan, targeting the two men reloading. The others were involved in a firefight with Jones and Cody, so fortunately they weren't under attack. Wilde scrambled into a limping run, clutching his shoulder as he went. Face wrenched in a grimace, he disappeared under the arches just as the two targets began returning fire. Will and Adams fell back behind the wall. Their distraction had worked. Crashing backward from exploding stone, Will cussed under his breath.

"Not the church!" He spat, no longer needing to be quiet.

Adams sneered and leaned back against the wall. Will offered a grunt before reassessing the next move. It would be too dangerous to go one at a time now that the men had seen their strategy. It would have to be a suicide run. Hopefully those two would realize this and make it to the arches of their own accord. Cody would probably be the one to suggest it. Jones tended to simply follow orders without thought, which was great for a soldier, but poor when leadership was needed.

Will looked back around during a lull in the gunfire and spotted Cody and Jones making fiery trails as they pressed into the archway. They were smart. That would save time. Their suicide run seemed to have worked. It was unlikely the attackers would expect another—at least not right away. In fact, those two running were all the distraction they needed. They couldn't hesitate. Will immediately smacked Adams on the back, signaling only one thing. The sergeant got the meaning, and they jumped into a sprint.

Unloading both pistols as he ran, Will saw the surprised expressions on the faces of his enemies. They brought their arms upward, trying to control their aim, but it was ineffective. The kick on those Tommy guns was too strong for taking proper aim; they were only good for strafing a target. Compounded by the oncoming blasts and the need to take aim, the gunners stopped shooting. It was all Will and Adams needed to skid into cover underneath the church arches.

Running out of breath, Will took a moment. Nerves buzzing, chest aching, and mouth dry, his eyes scanned the crew. Only Wilde was injured so far. They were mobilizing, organizing gear, and reloading weapons. Although the attack was sudden, and they were likely confused, they were well trained. Operating like clockwork with hardened expressions and military precision, he knew the group was prepared for the next chapter of this siege.

They took positions behind the arches, two behind each one, systematically returning fire on the barricade in front of them. No longer adhering to strategy, the enemy was just trying to hit targets.

Will managed to clip one of the gunners in the leg. He buckled with a cry and collapsed behind the sedan. The gunfire was persistent, and Will, for one, had only one round left.

With six against four and the enemy toting semiautomatic weapons, the only advantage they had was cover.

For a very fleeting moment, a thought fluttered through Will's head: *Who are these people?*

The firepower was overwhelming.

All the sergeants took accurate aim, but the parked cars served as an effective shield. Another round of reloading pushed Will's thoughts back into action. They'd seen at least three reloads, perhaps four. If the enemy was using fifty-round drums, that put this conflict at about a minute. That was an eternity in a firefight. More than that, and the tide would most definitely turn. There was no way they could hold this front for much longer. That gave them only a couple seconds to react to advance of the attackers.

Will knew they had to fall back. There was far more cover in the church, and it would draw the men away from the sanctuary of the vehicles. The decision was a costly one, however. It would bring the fight inside the church. If the others were prepared, that could amplify their forces. Many of the commanders were still combat-worthy, and some were legends. Will couldn't recall if they were well armed, however, and that was the risk he would have to take. They'd had long enough to take cover since the gunfire had erupted, so he'd had to have faith in his leaders.

"Fall back!" He ordered.

Adams and Cody were first. They fell into formation, shoulder to shoulder, firing their pistols in unison. Their cover provided an umbrella for Jones to duck behind. He pivoted on one foot and kicked the doors open with a stiff leg. It cracked under impact and flew open. The impact was their cue. The whole crew spun out of cover, keeping their guns blasting, and filed in.

Will was last. Watching the unfolding events stunned him for almost too long. Eight men equipped with semiautomatic weapons and wearing suits were charging forward. It brought a flash of the war into his head. Seawater and sand exploding around him. Rattling bullets in fog. Except these men were not an army fighting a war. He didn't know what they were, but they had skill and the combat reeked of wartime experience. Their charge was uniform and persistent. To avoid a complete barrage of bullets, he had to duck and dive in at the very moment he crossed the threshold of the church.

The dive wasn't a reckless one. He went to the side, dropping the unloaded pistol and holding the loaded one in a steady hand but arms outstretched. Tucking his head under, he rolled diagonally across his back into a kneeling position. In his next breath, he twirled on his knee and brought his pistol into a braced position pointing at the door, expecting an onslaught of suited men.

He was loaded, but no one came through the door to the church.

Will looked around inside. Jones and Cody were on the opposite side taking positions behind the back row of pews. Adams had gone farther into the aisle and was covered behind a pillar. Farther in, a dozen commanders were taking cover behind pews as well. Grand Master Sir Jackson was at the pulpit, unarmed. It was completely silent, but the tension was high enough to be almost audible.

It was too quiet.

There should have been a storm of bullets crashing through the church. The suited enemy should have stormed through, breaking off to the side as they advanced. Something was horribly wrong. It had already been more than five seconds. An eternity.

Then it all became clear. For the first time, Will's combative composure dissolved into near panic. He had just made a terrible mistake. They did exactly what the attackers wanted them to do.

By the time he shouted a warning across the church, it was too late.

# FOUR

ot even minutes before, the chapel had fallen silent as the occupants heard rounds of gunfire crack outside. Stunned, the men looked at each other, and in a moment of calamity, leapt to their feet. A few took guns from their jackets and found cover behind pews.

Dorothy's breath left her. Dizziness crept into her consciousness as she heard what must have been a full-on battle outside.

With each weapon that appeared in the hands of these mysterious men, the dizziness escalated. Bracing herself at last on a nearby pew, she looked up toward Mr. Jackson for some sort of direction. He stared absently ahead as if completely at a loss for what to do. The very real danger of the gunfire outside entering the church caused terror to grip her body. Looking around became even more difficult, and paralysis all but took over.

A couple of the older gentlemen stepped into the aisle next to her. One had a pistol drawn. The only weapon she'd seen of that kind was her father's hunting rifle, but she'd never even touched it, despite many offers from her father to do so. Being so close to the horrifying events escalating outside, she fell backward into a stumble as they came near. The only thing she could imagine was that the police were intercepting them. These men had to be criminals.

One overweight balding man gently took Dorothy by the arm. His gesture was in no way threatening, but his touch burned her cold skin. She reeled backward into another stumble, and he let go without a fight. A round pink face softened into compassion, eyebrows relaxing and brown eyes softening.

"We should find a safe place for you," he said.

"What in the bloody hell is going on here?" she barked.

"It isn't safe here."

The freeze was over. Now that terror clutched her, the will to survive took control. Sweat jumped out from her brow as her lungs clenched. Rushing energy broke through her body, splashing heat back into her skin. She clenched her mouth so tightly that she found herself biting her tongue. With the stance of a cornered beast, she glared at the man in front of her.

"Who are you people? What is going on here?" her tone was calm but carried a clear warning.

"Please, Miss Wilkinson," Mr. Jackson said from the pulpit, apparently having observed the conversation. "You must get out of here."

"I demand to know what is going on, or I will call the police." The calmness was leaving her voice. Inflamed eyes darted around, looking for anything she could use to protect herself. She saw only hymnals, prayer books, and candles.

"Miss Wilkinson, you must go to the temple," said Mr. Jackson. "The Grand Lodge of Quebec. Sinclair's letters are there."

"There is no time, go, now!" The large man said, losing his patience after she didn't respond to Jackson.

He reached to grab her, but she wouldn't have it. Survival instincts completely overcoming her motor controls, she opened her hand and laid a flat slap on the approaching man's face. The strike echoed through the air, and although she felt a shimmering thud in her wrist, it was quickly shoved aside by adrenaline. She twirled on her heel to run but was too fast and not stable enough. The heel snapped beneath her, and she fell tumbling to the floor.

At that moment the doors were broken open and hell poured through.

# FIVE

Bullets flew through the church, glass rained onto the floor, and blasts echoed around the vaulted ceilings. As Will completed his shoulder roll and finished reloading, he saw the true intentions of the oncoming army. Leaping to his feet he shouted, "Sir Jackson!"

The grand master was watching the battle with stunned silence. His aged eyes were sad, and he braced himself up on the pulpit, looking something like a priest. Casting his gaze to Will, his eyes no longer displayed fear. They were soft with quiet resignation.

For a very brief moment it all stopped.

The hairless man in the black suit stepped into the church with a single pistol in his hand. Will could see him clearly from his vantage point. He raised his freshly loaded weapon to put down the threat, but then the rest of the men stepped in and sprayed the church with their machine guns. Once again, Will had to dive for cover. This time he found sanctuary in a niche in the wall. Peering out to return fire, he saw what the bald man was doing.

His shot was straight and simple for a marksman. He let off a single round, and before Will could even scramble to his feet, Grand Master Sir Jackson fell backward as a bullet split his skull. Falling supernaturally slowly, he collapsed against the altar.

Time started again, and the moment accelerated into earsplitting warfare. The commanders were too slow to respond. They returned fire like caged animals, shooting uselessly back at the storm. Almost immediately three were shot down, and Will saw Jones take a series of bullets across his chest.

It was all falling apart. The fallback had failed, and now the army of well-dressed men was advancing farther into the church. Their gunfire ripped through the pews, cut open curtains, and toppled candles. Knights and sergeants returned fire, but they were no match for the onslaught. It was too little too late. They would all be dead soon.

*For what purpose?*

Desperation seeped into Will's consciousness. His arm kicked back with each shot, but his mind was no longer present. Growing distance separated him from the situation. After so many years of conflict with major societies and secret ones, he'd never before felt as if it was the end. This time he did. He'd die along with the knighthood by a torrent of assassins in a Canadian church. The prospect was a tragic anticlimax to the knighthood's legacy.

He closed the distance. He couldn't be complacent in their fate. As turcopolier, he had a duty to make sure his order was safe, and he'd die trying. Will repositioned himself, sprinting to a pillar next to the last row of pews. The men were advancing forward, so he'd soon be able to use his precious few bullets from behind—he had only six left.

After Will arrived at the pillar, he saw Master and Commander Sir Franklin just below him between the pillar and the last row of pews. He was a sturdy man who looked more like a military general than a bureaucrat. He'd known Sir Franklin for ten years now. He was just a baby out of college when he first met his mentor and joined his law office. He'd worked for Sir Franklin's crew since the thirties. Out of all of them, this was the man he respected the most.

Sir Franklin wasn't hurt, and he had a good spot by the pillar where he could easily take aim and provide cover. His white hair, cut short, was tousled, and fingers of sweat ran down toward his neck.

The mentor's eyes were wide and alert, and they brightened upon seeing Will.

"Do not let her die!" He said, enunciating each word.

It was a direct order, and it completely changed Will's outlook on the situation. He now had a mission, and it had come from the person Will respected the most aside from Sir Jackson. The mission may as well have been from God. The church, the safety of the Order, or the battle itself was no longer an objective.

There was only one woman in this church, and she was all the way in the back by the altar. Will saw her just before Sir Jackson fell. In open combat, civilians tend to duck and hide. Chances were that she was still there. He immediately mobilized himself, recalled the number of bullets he had left, and paused to put together a plan. The gun would get in the way. He needed speed, accuracy, and an exit. Peering around the pillar, he saw the corridors stretching back away from the rectory. There was surely a back door to this place. If not, there was a better place to hide.

It was ingrained early in his training never to question orders, especially those of commanders. They knew far more than any normal person could dream of. Will may not have known at that time why he was ordered to forsake his knights and commanders for an unaffiliated civilian, but he did know there must have been a very good reason. He didn't hesitate.

Launching into a reckless, albeit calculated sprint, Will jumped into the aisle, disregarding the exploding pews around him as bullets split the air. He ran in a slightly zigzagging pattern, forcing any attackers to take more careful aim. All his focus was on the first row of pews. Keeping steady and unblinking eyes ahead, he ran with all the strength he could summon.

There was a strafe on his tail, eating up the floor just under his heel. In the next moment, a simple gesture of the gunner's wrist would send the bullets all up Will's back. Aware of the danger, he pushed it aside. There was no time to change his direction now.

He saw his target. She was cowering behind the first pew, mascara streaking her face.

# SIX

Deafening sounds of war broke through Dorothy's strength. She sat with broken shoes, covering her ears, unable to peel her eyes away from the dead man that she had, only moments ago, slapped in the face. His heavy body lay in his own blood where a spray of bullets had dropped him. She'd never seen a dead body before, and she'd certainly never seen a man die. It was a hollow experience, ripping away her emotions into a placid disconnection where all she could do was sit back as an observer. The stranger's life fled from his eyes like a switch had been turned off. Never before had she realized that the depth of life was reflected in a person's eyes.

Too many thoughts rushed through her mind for her to make sense of anything. Images of her father, Bermuda, her sister Rita, her school and friends from the island splashed all across her vision. The disconnection began to connect again. Sitting in the presence of a corpse, she realized that this could very well be the end. Twenty-four years old and amounting only to being her father's messenger. She'd wasted her years on the beach, in the ocean, fishing, swimming … not doing anything important at all. Even when the war came to Bermuda and the allies built bases and launched airplanes, she blissfully ignored it, happy in her paradise. Her whole life consisted of her father, sister, and an island of tourists.

Her panic crashed heavily as she continued to stare at the dead man, while bullets whistled above. She remembered her mother. It was a distant memory, laced in fog and scratchy fragments, but a memory nonetheless. Her hair was tied up, her skin still wet from seawater. A smile and a wave. That day on the beach when she was five. That was the last time she'd seen her mother and the last time she felt like a child. Until now. Now she was a cowering child in the real world, clinging on to insipid memories, and instead of acting on surviving, she was lost in a flash of her life passing by as if it were a picture show.

A hollow feeling filled her stomach, and she felt her breathing go shallow. She was having a panic attack, and although she consciously knew that, she couldn't tear herself from where she was, nor could she stop the rushing memories. Fear paralyzed her, and this made her angry. She thought she was better than that. She thought of herself as an untamed Bermudan, raised in the jungle. In the outdoors. Surviving a dozen storms. Having sailed alone hundreds of times in some of the most notorious waters in North America. And here she was, crumbled and useless on the floor of a church, waiting for her death without so much as an argument against it.

The blasts increased around her, and her stomach nearly fell out as a bullet exploded into the pew above her. This snapped her back to reality. It was too close. No longer disconnected, the picture show of her life fizzled away. It was real and she was now there. A war zone was exploding around her, and she had the advantage of not having been seen yet. That advantage wouldn't last long. Getting up to her knees, she searched all directions for a way out.

Then, an unexpected man came careening around from the aisle. His gray fedora launched off his head as he made a high-speed turn toward her. A once-nice suit was now littered with specks of debris, and his blue eyes carried anything but panic. In fact, they were confident, belonging to a man with a silent mission.

She was too panicked to realize that she was the mission.

In the next instant, Dorothy found herself hoisted into the air by one of the man's arms. He grabbed her firmly but with delicate precision under her arm and stood her up. The move was invasive, aggressive, and terrifying. Certain this man was now going to take her life, the hollow gap in her stomach opened up again. She wanted to run, but she found herself frozen once more. Anger rising again, she found strength enough to push the man off her.

Then she recognized him. He was the one who'd greeted her at the door.

Dropping his hand to hers, he took her in a full sprint around the altar. He was getting her to run. In the next instant, she knew that this was the only person she could trust at the moment. For a reason unknown to her, he was trying to get her out of the church, and that made him her entire focus. She held his hand tightly and followed him through the debris of stone and wood by the altar.

Just then, one of the gunners launched into an attack after them. They'd been spotted, and it certainly couldn't end well. Bullets spat up broken pieces of stone just behind them. She wasted no more time looking at the situation and pressed forward into the darkness ahead.

The two ran into dark corridors. Several church offices behind the sanctuary flew by, and before she could register her surroundings, he'd kicked open a back door and the afternoon spilled on top of them.

# SEVEN

The fall air hit them as they ran through to the church grounds. Moistened grass and dew-tipped bushes were scattered presenting lazy obstacles. Keeping pressure on the insides of his feet to avoid slipping on the wet surroundings, Will was only slightly aware that he was dragging a woman with him. They were on the back side of the church, completely the opposite side from where he'd come in. He hadn't thoroughly surveyed this landscape because his crew was dispatched to do so while he secured the church itself. Another avenue, void of cars, stretched by, but he didn't know its name. An extensive garden stretched onward, offering a variety of other obstacles to run through. Glancing sideways revealed *Rue Ste-Catherine O*. It would be easier to run along the street than through the garden.

The human cargo tugging along behind was slow to veer as he headed toward the foggy street. Through the humidity he thought he spotted a parked car, and that would answer his current dilemma. She wasn't nimble enough to make the run. They had only moments to spare. In a few precious minutes, there would be gunners behind them looking for the escapees. He also suspected more gunmen were blocking the roads into this area. Or worse, local police. There would be no time to explain the urgency. He could only pull her along.

A biting urge to return to the church crept up. He couldn't help but feel he was abandoning his order and forsaking his leadership. It would appear as if he was fleeing the scene. It was a direct order;

there was no mistaking it. He was charged with getting this woman to safety—this civilian. Her life was held above his brothers, and as a soldier he couldn't question the purpose of the order. She must have known something very important—more important even than the survival of the knighthood. The glue that held the Temple of Solomon together were being massacred not yards behind him. It was worse than that day six hundred years prior, when his knighthood was all but eliminated on Friday the thirteenth.

They scrambled past the north wall of the church, and from behind it came a melodic huff. The concrete spilled onto the grass, and his dress shoes slipped as traction was taken away. Turning his foot toward the edge so the sole cut into the grass, he regained his balance and continued forward. Still the regular grunts and breaths echoed from behind. Cold fingers sandwiched in between his own struggled and jerked as their owner also attempted to keep her balance in the wet grass.

The fog was dense, but he could see Avenue Union. Not altering the speed or the manner in which he ran, Will pressed forward, pulling the woman with him. Squinting in the fog, he quickly took stock of the situation. Four cars were parked along the block: two were red, one was brown, and the last was black—or perhaps dark blue. Red was too conspicuous, and brown was just not his style. Opting for the black sedan, he lunged forward. Now with a goal in mind, he made every effort to reach the car as quickly as possible. The sooner they were in that car, the better. There wouldn't even be time enough to articulate this to his companion. In fact, during their sprint across the north lawn, Will didn't have the time to articulate anything at all to her.

He suddenly realized that she might think he was kidnapping her.

The woman yanked her hand from his. His realization came too late. Hauling her across the lawn into a sedan was going a bit too far. Reeling backward, he struggled to gain balance against the reactionary momentum of her release. Her eyes were wide, face pale. However, the widened eyes were focused and strong. She was frightened, but her fear wasn't controlling her. Perhaps in the last twenty paces she had been trying to decide how to handle her new fate, and suddenly she did with a simple explanation.

"I'm not baggage!"

This meant that she was a civilian. Years of fieldwork, several wars, and a revolution or two had conditioned Will to act and react with very little thought. Death, carnage, and violence went through him like an invigorating wind and charged him into immediate and instinctual action. Civilians thought differently. Often paralyzed by the sight of the unexpected, their minds tried to assemble the nonsensical, desperately attempting to salvage some sort of course of action, or at least a definitive role to play in the tragedy. Her mind was still in the church with the guns and dying men. Will's mind was already in the car and down the street as they accelerated toward safety.

The mission had stalled, and his plotting mind had been dragged to a jarring halt. He reversed his entire thought pattern and assessed their current situation, still yards away from the car he wanted to steal. Wanting with every fiber to grip the woman by the wrist and drag her into the car, he resisted. While it was vital that they make it to the vehicle and away from the scene, it was equally important that he gain her trust. Tossing her into the backseat like cargo would do little to accomplish that.

Taking a deep breath, he allowed his rushing mind to calm, and his searching eyes cautiously settled on hers. They were wide and unblinking. She hadn't lost her cool. Most civilians in her situation would be well down the path toward madness. Good posture and tight lips meant that her expression demanded a response.

"My apologies, Miss Wilkinson, but we must go."

It was all she needed to hear. Trust was established, at least for the time being. She needed to know that she wasn't a hostage and that he'd protect her. How else would a civilian know who to trust in such a situation? No longer yanking her along, they ran as a unit to the car.

The owner of the vehicle was either young or simply ignorant. Perhaps the former. It was unlocked and asking to be stolen. Will snapped the door open and allowed himself the privilege of glancing behind him. Blasts still echoed from inside, and their absence had yet to be noticed. His backward glance sent another spike of guilt into his psyche. He was about to completely abandon his men. It was an order. He had no choice.

He just hoped the master and commander knew what he was doing and wasn't simply saving this civilian out of chivalry. This woman must know something very important—something that would be the salvation of the Order. There was no other reason to send him. Will was the only one in the room who could be trusted not to fail—or to question his superiors.

His pause was dangerous, but it was long enough for the woman to climb into the passenger side. In fact, he waited long enough for her to glance up with a hint of worry in her eyes. Heart leaping, he jumped into the driver's side and took a breath. Nerves would do no good; he had to collect himself. The breath was enough to calm himself, and he immediately got to work.

Will started the Plymouth and in the next moment they were careening down Union. It was only after Will saw *Rue Ste-Catherine O* ahead that he realized why the city block was so vacant.

# EIGHT

The Barrister lit a cigar as he surveyed the carnage inside Christ Church Cathedral. Prone to perspiration, the bald man was aware he was likely glistening under the multicolored lights of the cathedral. He didn't act upon that until the battle was over. Reaching into his finely tailored suit, he found his silk handkerchief and dabbed it discreetly on top his head and down to the back of his neck. Replacing the handkerchief, he took another look around. Nerves bit him, and without realizing it, he gripped the back of his neck before rubbing his hairless head. It was a habit that he abhorred. For a man in his position to display nerves of any kind could be dangerous. Every time he noticed the gesture, he immediately brought his hand down, hoping no one had caught it.

It was no surprise he was nervous. No matter how carefully planned the mission, an assassination of any kind could go terribly wrong, and a massacre was exponentially problematic as well. So far, it had been a success, and the lack of activity outside suggested that the authorities had yet to catch on.

It hadn't been entirely successful. One loose end still had to be tied up.

Reaching under his shirt, he felt his familiar crucifix. It was cold to the touch but was still reassuring. It reminded him who he worked for. No matter what was expected of him and the ruthless way he handled sinners, it was indeed God's work, and the Holy See had sanctioned it. The heathens in this room were far from how they had begun. One of many orders meant to bring the Word of God to the infidels turned into a sacrilegious and disgusting distortion of faith, wherein they were caught worshiping false idols and committing sodomy. His own brotherhood had been kept pure through the centuries, but despite their best efforts, the heathens remained strong. This moment was a climactic victory in history. Once the loose ends were taken care of, the endless war would at last be over and the righteous would be the victors.

Those thoughts didn't lessen the blow of the battle's aftermath. Pews torn apart from bullets. Blood in all directions. Bodies cast aside. A hint of nausea crept up, but that was normal after battle. God's work wasn't always easy. He crossed himself. It was a habit that most of the society had, even those in the secret order of the society. Whenever a mission was finished, they paid reverence to God, remembering why they fought and whom they were putting down—enemies of God.

He paused thoughtfully after his prayer and then leaned down over the dead man before him. He saw vacancy in the aged eyes, and the man's gray hair was matted with fresh blood. The eyes were left open. It was as if the Barrister could see him as a living man leading the crusade against God. This man was the Order's most prominent enemy, and with a single bullet he'd been put down.

Cocking his head, the Barrister felt a sting of pity. The great Grand Master Sir Andrew Jackson had fallen too easily.

Looking up around him, he saw the dead or dying figures of the entire knighthood. A few scattered blasts echoed in the cathedral as the society finished off any who had survived. Their orders were clear. None were to be left alive. Yet one was. And a girl. A civilian. *Why in the name of the Holy did they have a civilian there?*

Now the far-reaching hand of the Church would have to reach into the outside world. He detested bringing civilians into their war. They were supposed to be protected by the Church. But it was his duty now, and it was the will of God.

Looking up at Sam Adams, the Barrister lifted an eyebrow.

"The others?"

"They won't get away."

"It'll be penance if they do."

Adams didn't let the effect of the threat appear on his face, but the Barrister knew very well that even the best of the society feared penance above everything else. No one wanted to look into the raging eyes of God. It wasn't a threat to be taken lightly, and until this moment, the Barrister had never said those words to his trusted minister. He had to make clear what was riding on this.

An eight-hundred-year war was finally coming to a close.

# NINE

"Shit!" Spat Will.

*Rue Ste-Catherine O* was blocked by three police cars, and a quick glance in the mirror showed that *Boulevard de Maisonneuve O* behind them was the same. The entire Montreal police force seemed to be there.

"The police," the woman offered. "They can help us."

"Those men are not police."

And indeed they weren't. The men in those patrol cars were no more law enforcement than Will was, or if they were, they had a very different agenda than law and order. They were hired henchmen. Blocking the city streets to allow a massacre wasn't exactly civic behavior. If they were apprehended, jail would be a blessing compared to their actual fate.

The sight of Will's stolen car prompted them to open fire, and with half a block left to go, it wouldn't take more than a second for their aims to become accurate. The windshield shattered, and the seat next to Will exploded. Policemen didn't simply open fire because a suspect was in sight, and Canadian ones certainly didn't. These men were armed soldiers and enemies of the Temple of Solomon. To what level, Will couldn't guess, but he would have to treat them no differently than he did the men in the cathedral.

Weighing his options was taking too long. He couldn't go forward, and he would lose momentum if he reversed. The car wasn't weighty enough to break through the barrier. The sedan would come to a clumsy halt, and they'd suffer head wounds from the impact. It would be ridiculous and careless to try to make it through that. They couldn't outrun them on foot. The whole point of stealing the car was to get away, and on foot they'd fall victim not only to the uniformed soldiers but to the barbarians in the cathedral as well. A catalog of other options spun through his mind, but he was left with only one.

# TEN

Thoughts were frozen in her mind, falling with no connection down into the depths of her consciousness. Vacancy enveloped her. A reaction to such displaced terror could only result in elimination of all emotions whatsoever. Dorothy saw the phantom next to her, steering the vehicle away from the authorities and onto the front lawn of the cathedral. Only moments before, a slaughter far beyond anything in her imagination had taken her into this whirlwind. Now she was a fugitive with an armed and very dangerous criminal.

It was difficult to breathe, and indeed, she wasn't sure if she remembered how. Life seemed to be some sort of fleeting fancy that had nothing to do with apparent reality. Only two days ago, she'd been enjoying the summer. Swimming in Harrington Sound with her sister. They'd planned to take a snorkeling trip the following day, had her father not sent her on this mission. If only he'd known what this business trip would entail.

Now she was in Canada. Kidnapped by monsters—associates of her father's. Victims of a bloody attack. Pursued by police. Words left her, followed by thoughts, and eventually any sensation at all. Her mechanisms fell apart, and she shut down.

She wondered how her father would handle this situation. Likely he'd quietly trust the man he was with because no other person seemed to be putting any effort into getting away from the situation. He'd ask questions later and then probably turn the fellow in to the authorities. That was what she'd do. If she could gather enough courage.

Gripping the armrest of the sedan, she watched as the kidnapper drove through a wall of bushes and leapt out onto another road. They were free of the police, but sirens were blazing, and the patrol cars were screaming into action. The man next to her said nothing as he tried to control his wild drive.

They were apparently going the wrong way on *Rue University* as he spun into a straight position. Three cars nearly collided into him before he screeched off in the proper direction where the one-way street split into two lanes. The police feebly followed, but he cut two corners and lost sight of them. They were once again crossing *Rue Ste-Catherine O*, but the barricade was now fumbling behind, trying to pursue his reckless maneuverings. Screaming left on *Boulevard de Maisonneuve O*, they were approaching a college campus. He stopped the car in a garage off *Rue University* and jumped out. When Dorothy didn't, Will looked inside.

Their eyes met. Her paralysis was clear, but an odd connection was made. She sensed in his eyes for the first time that he wasn't trying to hurt her. She was curious, and with a raised eyebrow she said, "Okay. I'm coming."

# ELEVEN

Will ran around the back side of the car. There would be plenty of time to make acquaintances later, but first he had to keep them both alive. Their trail would be easy to follow. Only a couple passes down University would tell the police that they'd entered this garage. The car would have clues in it, both for the police and the enemy. Not only could Will's identity be compromised, but the civilian's could be as well. If she were found out, whatever secrets the commanders wanted kept would be violated. He had to get rid of all the evidence.

A passing thought suggested that this driver kept extra gas. He kicked the trunk of the car with his heel. It was an aimed move, and all he needed to break the lock. Like a submissive child, the trunk gaped open, revealing a tire iron, spare tire, and gasoline can. It was his lucky day. The woman stood next to him with an openly confused expression, but he had no time to explain.

Popping off the top of the can, Will poured gasoline over the car before opening the door and spreading it all over the insides. He lit a cigarette, took a heavy drag, and tossed it inside. The woman stared, open-mouthed, but he didn't allow her time to react. Marching off into the garage, he grabbed her hand and took her with him.

"What in the name of God is going on here?" she asked.

Will didn't answer, but flinched at her expression. There was no time. He realized that she was trying to be assertive and take control of the situation, but this was no time to humor anyone. He had to complete the mission as efficiently and as quickly as possible. Her safety didn't necessarily mean her comfort, nor did it mean she'd be happy with the results. As soon as he was content with their security, he'd make her feel comfortable. For the time being, his obligation was to get her the hell out of there without a trace.

The proper maneuver was to disappear into the city. Unfortunately, he hadn't set up an escape route prior to the meeting and in fact didn't even fathom that one would be needed. Anyone with connections within the city was at that church, and all the other knights were so far overseas it would take a day just to get a cable to them. He was on his own and had to disappear into the city without the help of the Order.

It was back to the basics. He'd make them look like everyone else in a world of everyday people. All uniqueness would have to be discarded, and they'd need a location with throngs of people. The school was a good start, but an enclosed and informal location within the school would be ideal. His missing fedora was a big problem. Every man his age with his sort of dress sense wore a fedora. Not having one would certainly draw attention, especially to the trained eye.

A pillar of fire licked in the car behind them, but Will didn't turn to assess the damage. Instead, he took the woman by her hand as gently as he could and ducked inside a staircase leading to the first floor, where they slipped onto a somewhat busy street. Gathering his bearings, he saw the perfect location—the history museum.

Pointing at his objective, he looked over at his pale-faced and wide-eyed companion. She walked with him, but only because she clearly didn't know what else to do. Jogging across the street, the couple went inside the *Musée McCord d'Histoire Canadienne* as if they were tourists. This meant he continued to casually hold her hand. She seemed to accept the hint and walked with him. They were, for once, strolling. For a fleeting moment, Will allowed himself the pleasure of believing this was his actual life, walking into the museum with his sweetheart. The moment passed quickly but was invaluable to the ruse. Anyone who noticed the couple would assume nothing more about them.

The lobby was bustling with dozens of tourists who were luckily dressed similarly to them. Will purchased two admittance tickets and quickly but subversively went deep into the exhibits. Passing by the Eastern Woodland Indian Exhibit and the nineteenth-century Old West exhibit, he finally found a café tucked in the underbelly of the museum. They were camouflaged; no one would find them there or even think to look, especially if they were casual.

Will found a place to sit and offered his companion a seat before joining her. The two stared at each other for an awkward moment, and after coffee was ordered, he waited for the young blond-haired waitress to serve them and leave them alone.

Running his fingers through his greased hair, he once again missed his fedora. He would need to get another, or else he'd stick out. Men in the civilized world had a uniform, and he'd have to comply. Apart from that, he was accustomed to wearing one. It felt odd to be without it.

The events of the day caught up with him very quickly. He knew he had to speak to this poor civilian before she went completely mad, but he had a great deal coming at him. This day potentially marked the end of the Order. A very sophisticated hand had come in and eliminated it before his eyes. He alone had escaped, and only at the direct orders of a superior. If it weren't for Sir Franklin, he would be dead in that church as well. Instead, he was finding false sanctuary with an anonymous and young woman who seemingly had nothing to do with any of it.

Or did she?

During their moment of silence, Will came to a realization that he'd have to be completely candid with this woman. She was the only ally he had. Decades of harsh secrets would need to come to an end. The more he disclosed, the more his role in all this would manifest. From this time forward, she belonged to the knighthood in his eyes.

"I am sorry if I scared you, but we had to escape," he began. Hopefully she'd be willing to open up despite the circumstances.

"You're a fugitive. Those were policeman," she said coldly.

She was still stuck in a civilian mentality, and why wouldn't she be? She had no idea about any of this. As far as she knew, they were the mafia. Of course, that notion wouldn't be far off. In fact, they dealt heavily with the mafia, especially during the war when various influences in the United States were needed. Will worked with Lucky Luciano a number of times and expected to again in the future.

They were not the mafia, however. They were an ancient and reverent tradition that was on the brink of extinction. Even if what they did could sometimes be considered criminal, the efforts of the Poor Fellow-Soldiers were far above the law. No nation could determine its sovereignty.

He'd have to draw her out of the civilian mentality.

"The police wouldn't have barricaded roads so that men in unmarked cars could slaughter members of a legal and civil meeting."

"They were blocking the roads to stop the killers."

Will paused. It could certainly look that way. He knew, however, that traffic stopped long before the attackers arrived. It would be too difficult to explain. He had no further evidence for her. Even if they were policemen, and Will knew they weren't, they were still the enemy. Secret powers had ways of employing the authorities to do their bidding, even if that bidding meant the massacre of two dozen people in a church.

"Look, I know what this must look like, but you have to take my word for it. I'm doing this for your own safety."

"My safety? Your organization invited me to a damned bloodbath. You dragged me away from the authorities in a high-speed pursuit and promptly burned the car we escaped in. Sir, you are kidnapping me, and the second I find a way out of this, I will do so."

*Kidnapping?* Sometimes Will forgot how out of touch civilians were with the way things actually operated. Anyone in the secret world would have realized right away what was going on. This was a secret society war, and the good guys were the ones who saved your hide.

He sat back and studied her fearful yet stern and convicted eyes. Her short-cut hair was tousled, and she was still breathing heavily from running. A moment of sympathy crossed his consciousness. Whoever she was, she certainly didn't expect to get involved with this group.

"My name is Will," he said as he offered her a cigarette.

She looked down, suspicious, but then took one and leaned in for a light.

"The men at that church were high-ranking members of the Poor Fellow-Soldiers of Christ and the Temple of Solomon. I am a knight-protector and defender. The attackers ... frankly, I have no earthly idea who they were."

Recognition appeared on her face as her eyebrows rose. Glancing to the side for clarity and taking a hit from the cigarette, she leaned forward, "Knights Templar? You're Masons? My father is a Mason and he doesn't go around with guns lighting cars on fire."

Will wanted to run frustrated fingers through his hair, but he remained composed.

"You might be referring to the Masonic Knights Templar. The Poor Fellow-Soldiers became Masons in the 14th century after they were erraticated and have been operating as a secret higher order, outside of society and governments, for hundreds of years. We've worked to build and protect the free world."

"You are a ... crusader?"

Will shrugged. "We haven't been on a crusade in six hundred years. We've done a great deal of other things since then."

To the rest of the world, the original Poor Fellow-Soldiers died on Friday the thirteenth in 1307. Very few people, save for those initiated into the secret world, realized that the knighthood continued until the present day in secret and within the higher levels of the Freemasons.

The Crusades ended long before the Poor Fellow-Soldiers made a distinct imprint on society. It was, after all, their influence that impacted the modern world. It was their touch that gave capitalism the spark of life it needed. They were the forefathers of a liberal nation and the leaders of revolutions. They shaped the world they lived in. Yet all the world remembered them for was an ancient holy war spawned by the political aversions of an ancient pope.

"You expect me to believe that my father was doing business with medieval crusaders?"

He ignored the persistent and somewhat insulting reference to the Crusades.

"Your father? Who is your father?"

She paused, perhaps feeling she'd said too much. Her eyes suggested as much, glancing downward. She was a tough one, though, and recovered quickly. Only a highly trained man would have noticed her falter.

"Walter Wilkinson."

The name meant absolutely nothing to Will. It was no surprise. The Order conducted business all over the world with millions of people for millions of reasons. For all he knew, he could have just been some taxman in Miami.

*But why the meeting? The commanders all in the same room with the grand master for first time since Hitler's march into Poland?*

"Miss Wilkinson, you must understand that I am only a soldier for my Order. Most everyone initiated into the secret order is on a very strict need-to-know basis. I fear though that the entire leadership has been murdered. I must find out why. I need to know why you were at that meeting."

Nervous eyes danced away from Will as she smoked. "It was nothing really. My father just asked me to tell them about an upcoming storm."

"What upcoming storm?"

"A hurricane."

"Hurricane?" Will thought for a moment. "Hmm. I thought it was a metaphorical storm."

She blinked at him. "You don't know anything?"

"Need to know," he shrugged.

"Well, that's just swell. I suppose then I have absolutely no use for you."

"I'm here to protect you," he said. "And besides, I know *some* things. I know, for instance, that you and I are in very deep trouble."

"Didn't Sir Arthur Conan Doyle write a series of books about you? Smoking a goddamned pipe and solving mysteries, Sherlock?"

Will squinted at her. "Cute."

"Look, whatever your name is. I know two things: I was nearly slaughtered with a dozen men in a veritable war zone, and you are one of the men who should have been slaughtered."

"Sir Shakespeare."

"Come again?"

"My name is Sir William Shakespeare. You can call me 'Will.'"

This time Dorothy was squinting at him. "Look. Okay. Fine.

Thank you. I very much appreciate you getting me out of there. Now, I have to go and call my father."

"Call your father? What are you talking about? You can't call your father."

"Yes. I can. And I'm going to. Thank you, Mr... . Shakespeare."

She stood and Will stood immediately after.

"Miss Wilkinson, you can't go. You're with me now. I'm under orders."

"Really," she said with a smile. "Was the person who gave you those orders in that church?"

"Sit down," he said, more forcefully than he meant to.

She looked in his eyes ... judging ... coming to a conclusion.

"You have five minutes, Mr. Shakespeare. If I'm not convinced, I'm leaving. And if you try to stop me, I will make the loudest scene you've ever experienced. If the cops don't get to you first, then these fine museum patrons will."

He cocked an eyebrow but slowly sat down, conceding to her terms.

"Like I told you, I'm in service to the Poor Fellow-Soldiers. We've spent the last seven hundred years trying to bring human beings to their senses. Modern democracy, capitalism, the right to vote—all came from our work. Everything we do, every decision we make, is for the advancement of mankind, as is our mandate from God."

"That's very noble of you. And also ambitious. I'd like to know if you're also responsible for Santa Claus, New York in the autumn, and the production and timely distribution of rainbows."

"You aren't like most women," said Will with a furrowed brow.

She clicked her teeth and looked at her watch.

"Listen. Okay." Will sighed and rubbed his hands through his hair. "Okay, listen."

"I'm listening."

"The Order was disbanded in the early fourteenth century by an alliance between the king of France and the pope. Some of the survivors ended up in Scotland, where they took refuge with the Freemasons there. They adapted their rituals to be Masonic and established the Order and worked to spread Freemasonry. At that time, the Poor Fellow-Soldiers survived, but as a higher and secret order within the Masonic Knights Templar. This order has existed for hundreds of years outside of any government allegiance, to build a more perfect society."

"So?"

"So. Adam Smith, George Washington, Benjamin Franklin, John Adams, pretty much every single American founding father and all the philosophers from which the founding fathers took their ideology came from high-level Freemasons, and by extension us. The modern Western world was created upon Masonic ideals and philosophy that have direct traces to the our Order after we went into hiding."

She shrugged, her eyebrows raised. "Okay. Let's assume your group can take credit for modern civilization. What happened today?"

"I only have a hunch," he said under his breath.

"Why the meeting?"

"I assume because of this hurricane. Apparently something important is compromised. What were they asking about?"

"Bermuda," she said.

Will went through his mind and tried to call up anything that made sense, but nothing did.

"What's so valuable that they'd be worried about this storm?" she asked.

"I really don't know," he admitted. "But I think it's my job to find out."

"I thought it was your job to protect me."

"That too," he grunted.

"Fine. Who were these people who raided the church?"

Will shook his head. "That's my hunch."

She looked at her watch.

Sighing, Will said, "I think they were from the Vatican."

She frowned at him. "I may not be the first defender of Catholics, but it is hard for me to believe that Pope Pius sent men with guns to shoot up a church."

"Not as such," he said. "They're the military arm of the Catholic Church, probably operating outside the pope's knowledge, but under orders from their leaders in the Holy See. We've been at war with the church for centuries. It's my hunch that they somehow found out the entire leadership would be together under one roof and so struck."

"The Catholic Church attacked us?"

"Perhaps. But they were far too skilled and organized to be some hired assassins. Perhaps the Jesuits."

"Monks?"

"The Jesuits are much more than that. By that definition I'm a monk."

"If that's true, then how did they know?"

Will blinked at her. "Know what?"

"How did the bad guys know all the bosses were meeting in one place?"

The question smacked him across the face. It hadn't even occurred to him. It was a dark question full of impossible answers. He looked down, color leaving his face.

"What's the matter?" she asked.

"How did they know?" he repeated.

She looked at her watch.

"Okay, Will," she said, rolling her eyes. "Time's up. I understand that you're probably very important to society. I also get what happened today. I'll never forget what happened today. But it's a horror I want nothing more to do with. I've told you there's a hurricane coming. Now I'm going home."

She stood, but this time Will didn't. He said only, "You can't."

"Why not?"

"You're marked, Miss Wilkinson. They will find you. They will kill you. We are the only remaining survivors."

She sat down slowly.

"I need to get home. I need to find out what my father is wrapped up in. I need him to know what happened."

"I'll take you. I'll find a way," he assured her.

They sat silently for some time.

"How do I get home?" she asked.

"We can start with the lodge here in Montreal. We have a few squires there, but it's risky."

"The lodge?" she asked with a pale expression.

He nodded.

"The Grand Lodge of Quebec?"

Will looked up. *How does she know that?*

"Who's Sinclair?" she asked.

Will dropped his coffee mug, spilling it all over the table.

# TWELVE

Sam Adams felt hollow, as if his insides had been completely ripped out. Standing and sweating at the mouth of the church, he swallowed hard before going inside. The bodies were all laid out neatly on the church floor, and the "hired" police kept locals and the church proprietors out. They were very close to being successful, but then Will got away. Adams knew that Will was in a completely different class than the rest. He would be very difficult to track, but he had to be found. Adams' livelihood depended on it.

The whole operation was a precarious one. Very few managed to infiltrate the Poor Fellow-Soldiers, and although Adams had been successful in that, he couldn't have done it without the brutal training of the Barrister. Only through that man's work was he able to completely erase any evidence of his betrayal when looking his enemies in the eye.

It was a lengthy and grueling process. Already having devoted eight years to the project, Adams was in dire straits. If he failed, then a decade of his life would go down the drain and consequently his position in the society with it. He'd be as good as dead, or at least as worthless. He couldn't even think about the failure to the Church. No amount of Hail Marys could purify his inability to complete God's work.

He'd started, as most others did, as a priest. The Barrister was called that because he was one of the few in the society who was secular before he joined. He'd been a well-to-do barrister in London before the Great War. It was that war that turned him to God. One night deep in the trenches, he was under attack. As with millions of young men during that war, he was trapped in his own protection. Unable to flee the German advances, the Barrister hid amid the bodies of his fellow brothers. An enemy platoon descended into the trench, unleashing its weapons on the survivors. A German strayed and hunted down the wounded, finding the Barrister tucked under corpses. Their eyes met, and there was no doubt in the Barrister's mind that he'd be shot. Instead, the German's eyes softened, and he whispered, "You are touched by God" in perfect English. Moving on, as if in a trance, the soldier let him be, and the Barrister walked away, one of five from his brigade who survived.

Immediately after he was discharged, he joined the Lord's Service in a small Jesuit chapel on the outskirts of London. These particular Jesuits operated with the superior oath, so they recruited him, and many years later he climbed the ranks to become a superior rector. Most believed he was on the road to superior general appointed by the pope himself.

Adams' story was very different. Taking his oath at eighteen, he'd avoided any form of combat at all. In fact, he was entirely trained by the society. The superior rectors preferred it that way because the archaic ways of modern warfare were hard to remove from a person's mental vocabulary. The Barrister was a case in point. Very few operations went by without bullets being fired. It was all he knew. No, Samuel Adams was raised a priest and trained as a soldier of Christ. He'd been brought up in Georgetown as a minister. Recruited soon to the superior society after seminary, Father McKinley had taken a liking to the young man. His ability to blend into a crowd was his chief asset.

After training, Adams was immediately assigned to the Barrister's team for one purpose alone: to infiltrate the Poor Fellow-Soldiers. He had to create a new life and develop reasons for falling out of favor with the Church. The Barrister created an elaborate plot wherein he was excommunicated for practicing the last rites on a Jew. The stage was perfect, and he even got a little press out of it. The society had been following Will Shakespeare for the length of his career and had created the ideal scenario for the two to meet.

It was fall in Manhattan. Samuel Adams was destitute and disgraced. Living on the streets conveniently beneath Shakespeare's apartment, they often bumped into each other. After a few chats in a bar, Shakespeare took pity on him and gave him residence at a local Masonic lodge. All he had to do was shine, and over the next decade he'd become a trusted member of the Poor Fellow-Soldiers. Only a month prior, he'd accepted his vows as a sergeant and been given his name. No other Jesuit had gone that far.

And now the news was very sour. His lifelong effort was endangered.

The Barrister towered over the battle remains, his thick glasses hiding what his thoughtful eyes reflected. Running his hands over his bald head, he let out the sort of sigh that a worker gives after a long day's work. Glancing over at Adams, he caused the young man to jump inside.

"Barrister," he said.

The Barrister walked up with his head tilted. "Well?"

"Shakespeare and the woman got away."

A white flash exploded through his nose as the Barrister smacked Adams with the back of his hand. The blow was so startling Adams stumbled backward. In the next gesture, impossible to predict, the Barrister grabbed Adams' hair and brought him close.

"You've got penance. And when you are done, you will find them! I hope you understand that our entire cause rests on you finding them. You don't want to disappoint the Holy See, do you?"

The Barrister dropped him and returned to his work with the corpses.

"Don't delay," he stated.

Adams got up to his knees and pulled a dagger from his belt to begin penance, anger with the Barrister welling up inside. His zealotry pained him. He lost sight of the real path, the real purpose for the Poor Fellow-Soldiers. In his crusade against them, his will to completely destroy them, he'd forgotten what they held. The treasures they kept.

He whispered, gripping his rosary with his good hand. *"Ave Maria, gratia plena, Dominicus tecum, benedicta tu in mulieribus, et benedictus fructus ventris tui, Jesus. Sancta Maria, Mater Dei, ora pro nobis peccatoribus, nunc, et in hora mortis nostrae. Amen.*"

The Poor Fellow-Soldiers guarded the Holy Grail. He was so close he could smell it. This meeting ... this woman ... it was all about the Grail. It had to be. Nothing else made sense.

He stabbed the palm of his hand with a quick thrust of the dagger and then began another prayer as pain echoed through his body.

If Shakespeare and the woman escaped completely, the entire war would be lost. He had to find him. Follow him. Make him uncover the secrets of the millennium. This woman was the key. He had to move them, and he had to do it without the Barrister knowing.

Adams stabbed into his other hand, gripping the handle with ferocity, keeping his mind focused in order to repel the pain and began another prayer.

Shakespeare had been good to him during his initial training for sergeant. Still, with the title, he technically shouldn't have joined them on this assignment. Only through gentle persuasion had Will allowed him to go. His ruse worked so well that not even a tenured knight could recognize him. He had spent his months in Poor Fellow-Soldier training regularly reporting to the Barrister, and only one night previous had he received the order that the attack would ensue. All the commanders and the grand master in one building with a storm erasing their history.

It was as if God had handed them step-by-step instructions.

Guilt decorated his consciousness, but then, he was Catholic. Where would he be without feeling the pressure of his history of sins? Only through his work could he completely purify himself, and only through his faith could he move on with the knowledge that it was God's will he worked.

The throb in his hands radiated into his arms. He stood, crossed himself, and left the bloodstained church. Thoughts lined up in his mind, and he addressed them one by one. Trying to run through his catalog, he was looking specifically for a clue about where Shakespeare and the woman would go.

He knew why the commanders of the Poor Fellow-Soldiers were meeting. He knew where Shakespeare would go for asylum. And it was less than two kilometers away.

But first he had to find a safe place to make a call—far from the ears of the Barrister. There was some business in Bermuda that needed taking care of.

# THIRTEEN

The afternoon sun was setting early, as was normal for this time of year. Darkness was falling in, and it wasn't even quite four o'clock. It was a long walk to the temple, but both agreed it would be better than stealing another car, or even picking up a hard-to-find taxi for fear it wasn't a plant for the Holy See. The walk was quiet, and after leaving McGill, there weren't many other pedestrians. They passed many downtown landmarks, such as the Church of St. Andrew and St. Paul—a little too reminiscent of the church they were fleeing from. They arrived at the temple, roughly two kilometers from their starting point and directly across the street from another campus, the *Collège de Montréal*.

They arrived along *Rue Sherbrooke O*, or as Will knew it, Sherbrooke. Having walked the length of the Golden Square Mile district, Will wanted to spit out the taste. Many of these buildings had been built in the typical beau-arts style that the Canadians loved so much, even though most of the buildings were less than fifteen years old. The city was trying desperately to regain the population lost during the Great Depression and had therefore spruced up the lanes with maples and art-deco façades.

The temple they were approaching was one of these. Masterfully architected and now just shy of twenty years old, the *Grande loge du Québec* was a seven-floor limestone monolith dripping with Masonic symbolism. Designed by the late John Smith Archibald, known for his monumental structures and classical style, the building was not underdone. Masons from all over the country attended its ground breaking, and since it was the unofficial seat of the Poor Fellow-Soldiers, Will had been in attendance as well—though he had been much younger and not yet war beaten.

Since the lodge's move from Dorchester, about two kilometers back up into the core of the Golden Square Mile, the Grand Lodge had become much more official, tightly knit, and protective. The Poor Fellow-Soldiers trusted the temple to hold a great deal of its important documents. Poor Fellow-Soldiers gatherings, the few that existed, weren't held at the Montreal temple for reasons of security. Until today, it was the privately held Christ Church that arranged for their meetings, and before that the Dorchester temple.

The seven-story wall, featuring classical pillars and Masonic symbols, had medieval-style gates, cross-framed in iron. On either side of the gates were pillars holding bronze globes. *The porch of Solomon's Temple*, Will mused. The Boaz and Jachin columns symbolized the original Jewish temple, the framework from which the Order hailed its spiritual alchemy. Words above the door read "FIDES, VERITAS, CARITAS, LIBERTAS, and SPES": "Faith, Truth, Charity, Liberty, and Hope." Idealistic. Very Templar. It was a startling reference to the old laws of chivalry, which had waned since the world wars.

Dorothy was quiet upon their approach.

"Will they let me call my father?" She asked.

Will nodded. He pounded the knocker on the door and looked over his shoulder. It wasn't much of a stretch for the militant Jesuits to come here looking for them. Anyone with inside knowledge would know that this building was important to the Poor Fellow-Soldiers. This wasn't safe. Then again, the area wasn't secured for them. The cops would respond to an attack at the temple—no doubt. An open attack, anyway.

There was no immediate response to the knock. Will kept his back to the door and watched the darkening street and intersection. A few civilian cars. Not much else. The campus across the street was all but deserted.

An aged man at last opened the door. He was wearing a drab suit and unremarkable tie. His white mustache needed trimming, and he stood with a slouching hump.

"Yes, friend?"

Will turned, not recognizing him right away. Perhaps the tyler?

He extended his hand into a Master Mason's grip. The tyler responded by saying, "This grip demands a word, give me that word."

"At my initiation, I was taught to be cautious and to be private."

The tyler nodded and gave Dorothy a warm smile.

"Forgive me, may we talk in private? You may wait in our lobby where you will find some tea I've just brewed."

Dorothy nodded, seeming to be unphased by this and the tyler let them in. They entered the temple; the lights were on, casting brilliance over the polished black-and-white checkered floor. Arched ceilings were painted sky-blue with Masonic symbols appearing brilliantly throughout. Oak lined the walls and doors, and the open foyer, decorated stylishly with comfortable chairs and benches, ended at a ballroom. Double doors opened inside, and two dozen set tables stood, presumably ready for an upcoming dinner.

Dorothy took a seat and accepted tea from the tyler before he lead Will off into a room somwhere past the foyer. The tea was typical American, which was to say the plant was bruised beyond recongition to make it as bitter as possible, so she added sugar and waited. This cryptic behavior just witnessed would occur from time to time with her father and his associates. They never went past a certain point in her presence, but she knew it was some sort of coded question and answer process that was done, she supposd, to root out fake Masons before private matters were discussed.

Even knowing the process, she still allowed herself to be irked. Just another boy's club, excluding the woman—nevermind how important she happened to be to this situation.

They returned after a few minutes, the older man quite pleased with whatever transpired in there, and he eagerly offered Will tea before escorting them past the main double doors and through a ornately decorated corridor.

"I'm the grand tyler, Miss Wilkinson," he said as they went. "The name's Sutherland. You can call me 'Sully.'"

"Listen, Mr. Sutherland—"

"Sully."

"Sully," she said. "May I use your telephone?"

"Certainly," he said.

The three made their way around the ballroom and into a back office to the side of a backdoor corridor. The office was small, just enough space for a desk, three chairs, and a bookshelf.

"There you go, ma'am. All yours."

Smiling appreciatively, Dorothy sat down and punched in some numbers.

While they waited for her, Sully quietly said, "Everything okay? What brings you here?"

"Everything's not quite okay," said Will. "Really bad, in fact."

"Yes?"

"Jesuits," he said just above a whisper.

Sully raised two eyebrows.

"I'm all that's left."

The old man blinked at Will.

"Listen, I don't want to drag you into this," said Will, "so I won't go into too much detail. But the reason we're here is because Sir Jackson said we need the Sinclair file."

Sully squinted at him and sat back in his chair.

"The Sinclair file. There isn't a 'file,' per se."

"Do you have any idea what he may mean?" Will asked.

"Well, Sinclair's one of the protected lines, as you well know. But having to do with this temple?"

"Protected lines?" Asked Dorothy as she waited on the phone.

"Bloodlines," said Sully. "We keep track of particular bloodlines. Make sure the descendants are okay."

"Why?" She asked, then said into the telephone suddenly, "Wilkinson, Walter."

"Different reasons," Sully mused. "The Sinclairs, though, they are special. They come from the St. Clairs."

Dorothy listened, waiting on the telephone.

"Prince Henry Sinclair discovered the New World over a hundred years before Columbus," said Will. "He landed in Canada and started a Utopian society—what would become Montreal."

Dorothy blinked at him. "You're kidding, right?"

Sully shook his head. "No. Sinclair means quite a lot in this part of the world ... and with this lodge. Prince Henry built our city to be the perfect Masonic haven. Far away from the Catholics and the kings and whomever else wanted to get rid of them."

Will quietly nodded as Sully continued, "As a matter of fact, the Scottish Rite Masonry, the principles that this lodge was based upon, was essentially what became of the original Templars after they fled to Scotland."

Her eyebrows were furrowed, and then she was suddenly interrupted as she heard a voice on the telephone. "Say again?"

There was a pause, and the office remained quiet.

"Please patch me through," she said, looking a little pale.

"What's the matter?" asked Will.

"My father, he's been taken to the hospital. His pneumonia's gotten worst."

Will frowned, and the two men waited for her to connect with the hospital. The wait took longer than expected, so Sully turned to Will.

"Anyway, Sir William, we don't really have a Sinclair file. I mean, not a single document. I can't say what Sir Jackson was referring to. And frankly, since the move, much of the Dorchester documents have been taken away from the temple. There are too many outsiders here for them to be safe."

There was a pounding sound from the lobby.

"Another caller," Sully said and began to stand.

Will gripped his arm. "Be careful. Don't trust anyone," he said.

Dorothy waited on the phone, watching the two with curiosity.

Sully nodded and left the office.

"Wilkinson," said Dorothy into the telephone. "Walter."

She waited.

Sully's voice carried from the foyer.

They listened, waiting.

There was silence.

And a gunshot.

# FOURTEEN

*Not again.* Dorothy was horrified. The silence on the telephone was matched only by the silence following the gunfire. She stared ahead at the closed office door, mouth drying, heart palpitating. The world slowed down.

She dropped the phone.

Will snatched her hand in a firm and decisive manner and pulled her near. Then he approached the door slowly. He could hear his heart. In a gentle but swift gesture, he unleashed his pistol from its hiding space inside his jacket.

The corridor was quiet, and although illuminated by strong overhead lights, it felt dark. A heavy cough echoed from beyond in the foyer, followed by a groan.

"Shakespeare!" The hoarse groan warped into words. "Sinclair ... Roland Sinclair ..."

Dorothy watched an expression pass over Will's face, revealing conflict. She could guess over what.

"Let's get the file," she whispered.

He looked at her with stern dismissal.

"Quickly," she urged.

His eyes flinched. Whoever was out there had heard Sully as well. Dorothy already surmised that he was referring to a member of the lodge. Something she knew Will realized, and they both knew would dawn upon this murderer any moment now.

Will gripped her hand tightly and tugged as he bolted the

opposite way through the corridor.

A gunshot rang out and Dorothy's heart leapt. Like earlier in the day, time seemed to stop. She was being pulled downward as Will jerked open a door and they scrambled into a stairway. As she turned her head, she saw a nondescript man in a gray suit taking aim with a pistol as he marched forward.

There were two flights to the stairs and they exited into a basement. Blue carpet and fine Mason accents on bare walls met their arrival. Will ran with her through the vacant space and ducked into another corridor that led around a large central room—perhaps a ballroom. They flew down another flight of small stairs and broke through into a dimly lit, undecorated hallway that opened up access to several offices and storage rooms.

Will pointed at an empty office. "Take that cabinet, look for Sinclair. I'll take this one."

They separated, Will in one office and across the hall, Dorothy in the other. Heart fluttering and fingers stiff, she yanked on the filing cabinet. It was locked. Will realized it at the same time in his room. He rolled his eyes and then quickly snatched a pocketknife from his jacket. Dorothy watched from across the hall as he switched out the blade and pried open the mouth of the cabinet and then jammed his fingers in to switch the lock. He did the same quickly on the other three drawers and then whipped the knife across the floor, where it skidded into Dorothy's reach.

The sound of the basement door opening echoed through the corridor.

"Will? Will, buddy, I know you're down here. Looking for a file on ... who was it? Roland Sinclair? Master Mason? Third Degree?"

There was a pause. Dorothy looked at the blade and calculated if she had time to grab it—or if it was even worth it at this point. Looking to Will for guidance, she saw a look of confusion on his face that he visibly shook off as he returned to the cabinet, quickly searching for a file.

Dorothy lunged forward, grabbed the knife, and tried to duplicate his effort. It wasn't as easy as he made it look.

"Probably a knight too, for all we know. It is fucking Montreal, after all."

The echoing sound of another door swinging open crashed through the hall. Then silence. The murderer was quickly opening random doors, it seemed. Trying to find them.

She grunted, trying hard to pry open the drawer. It wasn't giving. She tried a different angle, stress clenching up her wrists and into her arms.

"Look, Will. I'm sorry. My boss, the Barrister. The man upstairs. He wants you gone. Dead. Bullet in the head like your friends at the church."

Will's eyes bulged as anger threatened to breach. He dropped what he was doing and stood up.

Dorothy looked at him surprised and mouthed, "What?"

He saw her reaction and shook off whatever it was that charged him before going back to the cabinet. Another door slammed.

"But listen. I don't want to do that because I know something that the Barrister doesn't. I know about the Holy fucking Grail. That's right. No amount of Vatican zealotry, ancient order rivalry, or political anything can stop the power of that. I know you know it too."

There was silence.

Dorothy continued to work on the cabinet. Something snapped, and the cabinet drawer reeled forward, knocking her over and toppling the cabinet onto the office floor with a loud crash. Buried under files, Dorothy looked up apologetically as Will rolled his eyes before leaping forward to help her.

The man knew where they were now.

Dorothy scrambled to her feet, and as she did, she saw the file. "SINCLAIR, ROLAND." Quickly, she ripped it open. Membership papers, signed contracts ... Will grabbed it and read the address on the top. He grabbed Dorothy's hand, scrunching the file in his suit coat, and they quietly jumped into the hall, proceeding into a storage room.

It was dark inside and full of high shelves stacked neatly with books and boxes. It could have been several hundred meters in area, if Dorothy had to guess.

"We have to get out of here," Will whispered. "I know him. He was one of us. Thought he was."

Dorothy frowned at him. "And how? We're in the basement."

"Good question," Will whispered back. They continued into the storage room, passing by shelf after shelf. "I was hoping for a basement window. Doesn't seem to be one."

"Or another way out," Dorothy observed.

The storage room door opened.

"Stop cowering around, Will," the man said. "I want to talk. You want the Grail, I want the Grail. Let's get the Grail. It's why the old bastards were meeting today, isn't it?"

"You're a son of a bitch, Adams," Will said suddenly, stunning Dorothy into a glare.

"That may very well be, but I'm actually not trying to kill you. I want what you want."

Will held up a finger to Dorothy, displaying confidence in something. Perhaps he had a plan. This earned him a roll of the eyes.

"And what is that? To take Miss Wilkinson back home safely? Because that's my mission."

"Will, come on. We're on the brink here. Nothing is in the way. It's within arm's reach. We just need to grab it. The Holy Grail, Will. The Holy Grail."

"That's what I want?" Will asked rhetorically.

"Isn't it?"

The voice was much nearer. On the other side of the shelf.

Will's arm bludgeoned the shelf so suddenly that Dorothy didn't know at first what had happened. With a closed fist he pounded a box on the shelf, and it launched off onto the other side, knocking Adams over into a surprised and stunned heap.

Next, Will jumped through the space he'd made in the shelf and landed smoothly on the other side in time to kick Adams back down as he began to stand.

Will sidestepped around Samuel Adams and kicked his gun away from him.

Now armed and towering over the bastard, Will tried to keep his military training in the forefront. Otherwise he would be emptying on him. The urge to slam his heel into the son of bitch's gut over and over was hard to overcome. He cracked his neck and kept his sidearm trained steadily at Adams's torso. Any movement, and he'd fire.

"Oh ..." Adams grunted. "Hi, there, Will."

"Why'd you do it, Sammy?"

"Do what? Come on, don't take it so hard." Adams slowly sat up, grimacing, indicating a pain in his neck from the fall.

Will was aware of Dorothy's presence, even through his anger, and so chose his words carefully.

"How long?"

"How long, what?"

"Sammy ... how long were you with the Jesuits?"

"From the beginning, Will," he said. His voice was edged with what was perhaps guilt.

Will shook his head. All those years. All that training. He'd been a mole from the start. He was built to infiltrate. His whole life was a lie.

"Do me a favor," said Will. "Don't follow me. If you do, I'll stop with police procedure. The gun will fire. Do you understand?"

"You think I'm afraid of that, Shakespeare, huh?" Adams said, suddenly angry. "I got much bigger problems, buddy. I need you dead. Except I don't want you dead. Come on, Will. The Grail."

"This isn't a crusade, Adams. You know very well that even if I knew what the Grail was, I sure don't know where it is. You're chasing a phantom."

"Bullshit, Shakespeare!" Adams barked. "There is one reason and one reason alone those men met in that church today. One reason." He pointed his finger at Dorothy. "Her! All we need to do is take her home. Then we find the Grail in a nice package underneath her pappy's property."

"You don't know that," said Will, softer than he intended.

"The fuck I do, Shakespeare! It's a fucking fact. Come on! All the king's men and all the king's horses together in one building. Why else would they be there? Why else would they fly her out here? Why else do they care about some tropical storm a thousand miles away! Think, Shakespeare!"

Dorothy started backing away, color leaving her face.

"The Grail's not my mission, Sammy," said Will, lowering his weapon.

Adams smiled. "Well, it oughta be. It's the whole reason the Poor Fellow-Soldiers exist."

"They don't exist. Not anymore," said Will, letting his sadness out in the tone. "And I have you to thank for that."

He looked over at Dorothy and waved, defeated, toward the door. "C'mon."

As they were walking out, Adams said quietly, "It may not be your mission, Will. But it's mine. I have people behind me. I have people in Bermuda."

Will looked up sharply before catching Dorothy's startled and enraged face.

She marched forward, but Will held her back. "What do you mean by that?" she asked.

As Will kept her from approaching Adams, who was now standing, she barked louder, "WHAT DO YOU MEAN BY THAT?"

"Nothing," said Will. "Come on. We have to go."

He picked up Samuel's gun and turned back to him. "You touch her family, Sammy, you'd better hope God still listens to your prayers."

Adams held up his recently bandaged hands. "Already prayed today. He doesn't."

Will winked and then knocked over one of the shelves, which resulted in a domino effect, knocking over all the other shelves. Piles of boxes flew down and buried Adams.

His voice sounded from below the rubble. "I'll give you a head start, then."

As they jogged across the foyer, Dorothy gasped at the sight of Sully, holding his stomach, lying in a violet lake of his own blood, pale and slowly moving. Will let go of her hand and ran up to him. Dorothy all but forgot about the incident moments ago and the open threat to her family.

"Ah ... Sully. I'm sorry I dragged you into this," said Will just above a whisper.

"You have to see Roland. Even ... if you ... drag him into this."

"We'll go."

"You can say the prayer, can't you, Poor Knight? Before you go?"

Will quietly said, "*Sancti spiritus adsit nobis gratia. Maria, Stella maris, perducat nos ad portam salutis. Amen.*"

Sully smiled weakly. "I meant the Lord's Prayer, you heathen."

Will chuckled, then whispered, "*Pater noster, qui es in caelis, sanctificetur nomen tuum. Adveniat regnum tuum. Fiat voluntas tua, sicut in caelo et in terra. Panem nostrum quotidianum da nobis hodie, et dimitte nobis debita nostra sicut et nos dimittimus debitoribus nostris. Et ne nos inducas in tentationem, sed libera nos a malo. Amen.*"

Sully looked peaceful, "Yes. That's a good one."

Then he passed.

# FIFTEEN

They were quiet as they drove Sam Adams' car down Sherbrooke. In just a few short minutes they would be in the Westmount district, driving by beautifully architected homes, vast green spaces, and incredible views of Mount Royal and its cascading auburn trees and pastured hills. The setting sun sprinted across the hills as the Canadian sky turned from gold to turquoise.

"How are we going to get me home?" Dorothy asked quietly.

Will shook his head. "Working on it. I have an out in New York if we can get there."

"What was he talking about? The Grail?"

"A treasure hunt, Miss Wilkinson. Not on my mind."

"Then why are we going to this Sinclair's house?"

Will looked at her with a raised eyebrow and an exhausted expression.

"We have no other place else to go."

She smiled at him, and he returned the smile, shrugging. "I don't."

"What about Adams?"

"We'll need to get Roland out of his house. Someplace safe."

"And where's that?"

Will paused. "I'm hoping Roland can help with that."

He took a side street from the boulevard and after a few turns ended up at the foot of a very large single-family home. It was colonial design, with red brick, white columns, and white-bordered windows. Large red maples blocked most of the view. Parking on the street, Will stopped the car and gave her a "ready?" look.

The two walked cautiously up to the door. A porch light was on, but there didn't seem to be any other indication anyone was home. Will rapped on the door. After a moment, it was opened by a short older lady wearing an apron and drab-colored dress. She squinted through her thick lenses.

"*Oui?*"

"*Bonsoir, madame. Est Monsieur Sinclair à la maison?*"

"*Qui êtes-vous?*" she asked.

Will sighed a little and scratched his head.

"*Nous avons été envoyés ici par un ami du temple maçonnique,*" he said.

She nodded with a suspicious look on her face and then opened the door for them.

The house was elaborately decorated with fine chandeliers, woodwork, and beautiful tile. They could see into the dining room from the foyer, where twelve seats were set under a delicately embroidered cloth.

She gestured to a love seat in the foyer and said, "*S'il vous plaît, attendez ici.*"

Will and Dorothy sat down.

There was a long, awkward silence after the woman left them and went up the staircase.

At last, a large older man wearing a white cotton bathrobe and carrying a martini glass walked down the stairs. His long-lost hair was replaced with gray wrinkles, and the laugh lines around his eyes were further accentuated when he approached them with a large, wrinkly, open-mouthed smile.

"*Bienvenue, chers amis. Puis-je demander pourquoi vous appelez?*"

Will stood and shook the man's free hand. "Good evening, monsieur. I am William Shakespeare of the Poor Fellow-Soldiers of Christ and of the Temple of Solomon. This is Dorothy Wilkinson."

"Poor Knights?" he said, his accent thick. "Shakespeare? I recall knowing your name. Years ago. You were in Vietnam, yes?"

Will nodded. "Yes."

"I was stationed there too, before they sent me to work at the lodge. Well! To what do I owe this pleasure?"

"Monsieur, I'm afraid we have nowhere else to go, and I regret bringing you into this ..."

"Into what?"

"Monsieur, you are not safe here. Let's relocate you and your family."

"No family here. Only Ursula." He thumbed back behind his shoulder and made a face.

"Please, monsieur. We'll explain on the way."

"No need, Poor Knight. We are safe here, come. I'll pour wine. Or if you like, I have more of this ..." he pointed to the glass, "... whatever this might be. It's in Russian. The letters look upside down to me."

"Please, monsieur, it is not safe. Jesuits have taken many lives already."

"Jesuits? I hope you don't mean the scholarly bunch with all of the universities?"

Dorothy snorted in spite of herself.

He waved his hand. "Do not worry, Poor Knight. I'm not concerned with Jesuits. Even the superior ones. And besides, by all written accounts I live in Pasadena, California."

"Not your lodge file."

"Well, not my lodge file, no. But I'm a Master Mason! I know better than to lie to my lodge."

Will gave Roland a skeptical look.

"Very well, come. We will talk. But you need to be proven. Miss ... Wilkinson, is it? Come."

The robed man escorted his guests into a den off to the side of the dining room, where there were well-upholstered leather chairs and couches and a full bar to the side. He sat on the couch, bare legs popping out of his robe.

Taking a sip of his martini, he pointed to it with a questioning expression.

Will shook his head and was about to speak but was surprised when he heard Dorothy say, "Yes. Please."

Roland grinned and stood to pour Dorothy's vodka and vermouth into a shaker. After serving her he said, "Forgive us, as we must take care of our secret handshakes and endlessly senseless questions to one another."

"Knock yourself out," she said taking a long pull of her drink.

Will and Roland retired to an office adjacent to the study, where Will passed him the Poor Fellow-Soldier squire grip, happily he returned with a confident question.

"This grip requires a word."

"It does not," Will said begining the test.

"I was taught upon my initiation, that upon recieving the word, it should be imparted to those that ask," he responded.

"There is no such word for this grip."

"That does not satisfy me."

"Satisfaction cannot be had in this matter."

"Give me the word."

"I cannot."

"Then I must have another grip," Roland said.

"There is no other grip to satisfy this obligation," said Will.

"Then this obligation does not exist," said Roland.

"Except in the presence of Solomon, King of Israel, Hiram, King of Tyre," said Will.

"Do you have the number?"

"I do," said Will.

"Will you dispose it?"

"I will halve it," said Will.

"Then begin, brother."

"No, you begin."

"Begin you."

"Thir," said Will.

"Teen," finished Roland.

Then Will smiled, "Pleasure to meet you, squire."

"Let's drink," said Roland who patted him heavily on the back.

They returned to the study, where Dorothy had put an impressive dent in her martini.

"What happened then, Poor Knight?" Roland asked sitting down.

"There was a meeting," Will sat next to Dorothy. "All the officers were present, and as I soon learned a traitor had informed heavily armed enemies. They came in and slaughtered everyone. I can only assume they are the in the Superior Society of Jesus."

Roland stopped mid-drink and raised both eyebrows. "Slaughtered everyone? Except for you?"

"And the traitor," added Will. "They followed us to the temple, and I'm afraid your tyler has been killed as well."

"Sully?" Roland contemplatively poured Will's drink and handed it to him. "A dark day, indeed."

"So you see, they know your name, and they know we are seeking you out."

"They won't find this place, Poor Knight. The address is only on that lodge record. The one you took with you, I presume."

Will nodded.

"Very well, then."

Will took a drink and for the first time that day relaxed his shoulders.

"May I ask why it is you came here?"

"The Grail," said Dorothy.

Will looked at her, eyes wide.

"Actually, monsieur, we need to get Miss Wilkinson back home to Bermuda."

"Both sound fairly impossible," said Roland under a grin.

"Forgive me, monsieur, we haven't had time to talk about this," Dorothy said, "so I will speak openly. The men ... Will's bosses ... they met this morning about a storm hitting my father's property in Bermuda. Something of value is there, and it will be lost with the tide. Will is on an absurd mission to 'protect' me—which he has done a bang-up job of so far. I don't care about his mission. I need to find out what it is that is on my property. And whether my family is in danger because of it."

"Bermuda?" He thought. "I couldn't say, mademoiselle, any more than this man right here can. But there is something I can help you with."

He stood up and wobbled over to a painting of medieval ships in a battle on the high seas. Pulling the painting forward on hinges, he revealed a safe. He opened it and brought over a binder with some very old documents.

Setting the binder on the table and taking a pull from his martini glass, he opened it and found an aged hand-drawn map of Nova Scotia. He pointed to an island.

"Oak Island is one of the sites of the first European colonial landings."

"I'm rusty on history, but wasn't that in the Caribbean?" asked Dorothy.

"Modern history suggests that Christopher Columbus was the first European to the New World, but history is wrong," said Roland. "The first landing occurred a hundred years before Columbus and by a Scottish noble. He was a Knight Templar. And one of the few lines that survived. And my great-great-great-great … my ancestor. Prince Henry Sinclair. He landed in Nova Scotia in the year 1395. He had very precious cargo with him and buried it at what is now called Oak Island, where he built a fortress to protect it."

"What is this treasure? Gold?" she asked.

"I'm only a Master Mason, ask my fratre here."

"The only ones who knew what the treasure was were murdered this afternoon," said Will.

"Obviously, the men who shot them must know," said Dorothy.

Will hesitated. It was indeed possible but highly unlikely. He could accept a traitor among the brothers, but not the commanders. If it was, in fact, the secret operations of the Society of Jesus, the Vatican certainly knew about the treasure. It would make no sense for them to be after it now, however. They had all the wealth in the world. Unless the treasure somehow compromised their position.

"They destroyed the easiest way to the treasure then."

Dorothy looked back to Roland. "You're wrong about that Henry fellow. Columbus discovered America."

"That's what the Vatican would like you to believe," smiled Roland.

"What do you mean?"

"Columbus was a publicity stunt. Not only did Europe know about the New World; there were accurate and established maps of the entire continent. There were even others here before Sinclair, but he was the first to make a colony."

"What about the world being flat?"

"Nonsense. Only the uneducated and superstitious would have believed that in 1492. Columbus knew right where he was going. So did Sinclair a hundred years before him. The difference was, Sinclair had the maps far before the Vatican. This would have been an extremely valuable document. Columbus had bad maps. But he had them."

She thought about this for a while. Although what Roland was saying was common knowledge for Will, he realized this wasn't the material taught in schools. Her British accent and Bermuda home suggested she'd received proper colonial education—perhaps even a private tutor. They would have had no idea who Sinclair even was. They certainly wouldn't have known that he was the father of the modern Poor Fellow-Soldiers and the genius who brought the most important treasure in history to safety, out of reach of a corrupted Vatican government and its countless national henchmen.

Roland pressed on and opened more pages of the binder, pointing to aged documents.

"The son of a crewman, Antonio Zeno, wrote about Sinclair's voyage shortly after his death in 1400. They included a full account of the trip to Greenland and then Nova Scotia, complete with remarkably accurate maps and descriptions of the native Micmac tribe. Relics of the original colony were still quite visible in the form of the Newport Tower and stone carving that locals called the Westford Knight.

"In fact, evidence of Sinclair's landing is everywhere in Nova Scotia. An ancient graveyard used Templar symbols such as pentagrams and the famous Crusader Cross. Even the name *Nova Scotia* was Latin for New Scotland, an appropriate name for a Scottish noble trying to create a Utopia in the New World.

"Sinclair's son, William, constructed the Masonic icon the Rosslyn Chapel and built in carvings of American plants ten years before Columbus even set sail. The chapel was actually created as a massive red herring to divert attention from Oak Island, where the treasure was really kept.

"The Scottish colony was no secret to Columbus, and, in fact, he himself was a Templar working under guise. He donned the Templar cross on his sails and used derivative maps from sons of Antonio Zeno. His was a secret Templar mission, so secret, in fact, it was blessed by the Vatican as an endeavor from Rome. Columbus was picking up where Sinclair left off, looking for more places to establish a Masonic stronghold in the New World.

"His Spanish counterparts, however, had a different, more earthly agenda in mind, and even in the earliest days of colonial America, the Templars fell into conflict with Spain. The Templars, through the Masons, would eventually have their idealistic nation, but it wouldn't be because of Spain, it would be through a revolution against Britain many hundreds of years later."

Dorothy clicked her tongue. "That may be a matter of opinion."

Will smiled and then laughed.

"Is it the Grail?" she asked Will. "Adams seems to think so."

"He wouldn't be the only one. A lot of people think something special is on Oak Island."

"Something special *is* on Oak Island," smiled Roland.

He flipped more pages and then pointed to a map. "Treasure."

"People have been excavating there for decades," sighed Will. "There's nothing there. The Order'd have moved anything important the moment the colonials came in."

Roland shrugged. "Maybe they aren't looking in the right place."

"What docs this say?" Dorothy askcd, looking more closely at the map and trying to decipher the handwritten scrawl.

"Directions, mademoiselle. And notes about where the booby traps are."

Will squinted at him and then leaned forward to look at the map.

"Amazing ..." he said. "Is this ... ?"

"Prince Henry's treasure map," Roland grinned.

Will and Dorothy looked at each other.

"If you want to find out what is so special about what your father has in Bermuda, you go to Oak Island first," he said. And then, pointing at Will, he added, "And if you are the last remaining Poor Knight, you must go to Oak Island. Orders or no."

Will's heart escalated as he looked at the 600-year-old document. *The Holy Grail ...*

Oak Island, New Brunswick
September 7, 1947.

# SIXTEEN

T he dark highway droned underneath them. Only faint shadows of towering evergreens could discern their movement. Cloud cover had taken away any chance of stargazing, and with their mood, the stars would be unnoticed anyway. AUT-20 stretched far to the east, and Montreal was all but a distant memory. There was very little conversation between the couple, save for some obligatory comments as they stopped on their way out of town for decent walking shoes for Dorothy and a new fedora for Will.

Although they hadn't spoken much, it was at least determined that Dorothy needed to go on this hunt before she went home—at least for the safety of her family. They were somehow in this together, although neither one could imagine why. Tensions subsided a couple hours outside of Montreal, and it wasn't long into the drive before they stopped exchanging words. Dorothy wanted to know how far Oak Island was, and after a shrug Will estimated it would be about ten hours. That was two hours ago.

Will rather appreciated the silence. He had many thoughts to gather. Now that the mission had been temporarily successful, he could reflect on the events of that afternoon and collect them into some sort of meaning.

"Why did you get the name?"

"Name?" he asked, startled by the sudden break in the silence.

"Shakespeare."

"When you join the Order, you forsake your entire identity and take on a new persona, completely unrelated to your old life. They give you the name of a beloved Poor Fellow-Soldier. I was named Shakespeare. Never learned why exactly."

"If everyone gets a Templar's name, won't your organization eventually run out of names?"

There was a long pause before she couldn't hold it anymore. Maybe it was the stress of the day, the absurdity of their conversation, or the seriousness in his tone, but she released a guffaw that filled the entire car. Laughing uncontrollably for an uncomfortable amount of time, it finally tapered into a snicker.

"I'm sorry, it's just that ..."

"You think it's crazy," he completed her thought. "I don't blame you."

It was all he said. No further justification, no further comment. For a moment she felt bad.

The knowledge that her father and sister might be in danger kept her on this trip. If the property was the thing that put her family in harm's way, then she wouldn't care about this treasure hunt. In any case, she knew Will was her ticket back to Bermuda. She couldn't go back to Montreal, not after all of this. This William Shakespeare would be her ride.

They had a long time to go before the mysterious Oak Island would finally appear in the dark scenery ahead of them. To pass the time, she considered asking more questions about his crazy notions of history, but she held back. She didn't want to bombard him with more laughter.

Not too much later, Will pulled over and Dorothy took the wheel. He wanted to review the documents Sinclair had given them more closely. It was silent from that time on. Will used a flashlight to read each page closely and occasionally looked up to overcome overwhelming car sickness.

# SEVENTEEN

Oak Island was lit with electric lights that could be seen from down the bay. Pulling into Chester at night meant that those lights were the brightest on the coast. Will was as surprised as Dorothy, but not because he didn't know what the contraption was. No one had been excavating on the island for ten years, and yet there was a massive crane and pulley system, lit with floodlights and surrounded by trucks and tents.

He cursed, and Dorothy raised an eyebrow at him.

"Let's hope they had a late night."

Checking his watch confirmed it was still only three-thirty in the morning. Not even the most eager started that early.

"Who are they?" Dorothy asked, now recognizing the contraptions as they came closer.

"Treasure hunters."

"I thought this was a secret."

Will shrugged. "The promise of fortune makes people very persistent."

As they drove down Lighthouse Road, the hoopla surrounding Oak Island seemed somewhat anticlimactic. It was a humble hill of shrubs and sand connected by a man-made bridge. Various rocks created several coves and bays on the small plot, and the largest feature was a massive excavation at the southeast end of the island. The notorious "Money Pit."

Heaving a sigh, he directed Dorothy to park the car on the edge of the island and turn off the engine. Tapping the steering wheel absently, she waited for him as he considered the best approach. They weren't going anywhere near the Money Pit; however, their hike would take them close enough. It was still cold, and they had no swimwear.

"I'll be blunt," he said. "This is no place for a lady. We'll have to swim and go into ancient underwater caves. If the treasure hunters find us, we'll have to get away with no clues as to where we were or why. Tell me now if you aren't up to it. You can stay in the car and keep watch."

"Sir Shakespeare, if you honestly think I'm going to let you go treasure hunting without me, then you really are mad."

She got out of the car first.

"So mote it be," he whispered under his breath.

Incensed that Shakespeare said the words "This is no place for a lady," Dorothy sought not only to prove that women could be here but that it was better that they were. She'd grown up in an island colony, not some farmhouse in Nebraska. America may have its proverbial undies in a wad over the rights and privileges of women, but British colonies sure as hell didn't. A woman worked just like a man, and, lest men like Shakespeare forget, it was the women who ran their bloody country when the U.S. troops were overseas.

This was no time to discuss it. Much more important matters were at hand, and despite Will's demeanor, she didn't believe he meant harm. He was only trying to give proper warning. After all, she was wearing the business suit she'd bought for this purpose. Had her father convinced her not to, she'd have been wearing slacks and a breathing top—like she always did. Often on the island, she wore nothing but a bathing suit. Stuck in recently purchased pumps, a long skirt that was tight around her hips, a button-up top and jacket, she felt more like a Cosmopolitan advert than a Bermuda Wilkinson. With a hat to boot, it was no wonder Shakespeare had warned her of their upcoming adventure.

She'd overreacted, perhaps, but the whole situation seemed wrong. Was this man really trying to protect her, or was she simply being used to get to the property? She'd play his game, but only because it was clear he thought she was naïve. They'd find what was on her property. She'd then give the treasure to the rightful owner, her father. Anything on land he owned belonged to him, and no ridiculous private club of history conjurers and criminals would take her father's property from him.

*We'll see what sort of place a lady belongs, Sir Shakespeare.*

# EIGHTEEN

The Barrister was enjoying his cigar. Sitting back in the reclined passenger seat of his sedan, he took a few very relaxing puffs before then savoring the taste of it in his mouth. A cloud of smoke enveloped him like cotton. Muscles underneath his neck began loosening. It had been a rather difficult day, although they'd been mostly successful.

He could have taken time to bask in the success, taking into account that this was the first time in six hundred years that the righteous had disbanded the heretics. His charge from the Holy See finally realized, he could have used this cigar as a celebration for thousands of years of strife coming to a close at his hands. But he knew better.

One of them had escaped, and when one was left, the whole thing survived. They'd seen it time and time again. All too often, the Church would finally take down the heresy, and one weasel would spawn a whole new society. One of those societies had become the United States of bloody America. Anyone left was a dire liability, no matter how insignificant.

And this one was not insignificant. He'd taken the monastic oaths of the Knights of Justice. No simple man could make it that far in the Templar society. He had guts and wits. The stuff leaders are made of. He already had a reputation, and he had his spy nervous.

The civilian was another matter. She only remained a threat as long as the treasure remained intact. Once the storm blew through and the deed was done, she and her family could be left alone. They should be. It wasn't his intention to make the innocent pay. It wasn't her family's fault that the surviving Templars put treasure on their land in the sixteenth century. Even if her family had the knowledge, it was no matter. Without the Poor Knights and the treasure, the knowledge was meaningless.

The Barrister took a thoughtful pull from his cigar. A job well done? Not so. A job not nearly completed. No strings were to be left untied. No messes left to be cleaned up. No evidence of the deed at all. Despite his own beliefs, the Barrister lived in a secular world, and he knew that. Not even the pope ... not even the superior general of the Society of Jesus understood the full significance of their mission. Only he did. Even if they had inside information, the significance of the war was rather downplayed by the Vatican. A weak pope. A weak superior general. The truth would spread throughout history. 1947 would go down as the year when the real Christians triumphed.

That would only be true if this Shakespeare were caught. The Barrister had his doubts; however, he knew that the power of Christ was strong with Sam Adams. Despite adversity, the young man had been able to infiltrate one of the most protected and secretive societies in world history.

It was a bloody shame. This whole arrangement. Two societies, far from the eye of the general public, waging war over the centuries. The Barrister well knew that he was a simple link in the chain, but his cause was just as significant as any worldwide movement. He was a leader of a legitimate society charged to do God's work by the pope. He cared little for human politics and not at all for simple drama. It would take far more than a shout or even a murder to raise his eyebrows.

Now looking down the barrel of an almost-empty gun, the Barrister saw the most notorious enemy of the Catholic Church completely eliminated. No longer would there be hysterical representations of history, no longer would there be secrets among the pious, and no longer would there be a secret war ravaging across the world throughout history.

This secret conflict could finally close. And these so-called "secrets" the Templars held would be obsolete. Never again would some radical left-wing nutcase shout on his pulpit about the evils of the conservative world. Never again would there be discourse on the secrets the Vatican held. Imagine! The pious demanding answers from the Church? What sort of world existed in a paradigm where religious consul was, in some way, accountable? Didn't these people realize that the will of God could not be understood? Didn't they realize that despite all the structure, God only wanted mere happiness? So what if prior administrations in the religious realm of Christendom committed crimes? Wasn't it important enough that the message was released all over the world?

These infidels held horrible secrets. It wouldn't be the Barrister who destroyed them. It wouldn't be any nation, ideology, or event. In fact, it would be God Himself. A hurricane was coming to destroy all those things the Templars considered sacred. The pagan infidels would, at last, have their day.

His cigar couldn't be enjoyed. Too much work still needed to be done. He couldn't relish the near-victory of the society because it was not a victory. William Shakespeare had escaped. The result could not be undone. Instead, he had to bear the steady reports and more work. As a constant reminder of his shortcomings, various people reported on the progress of the failed mission.

The most annoying of all was the infidel and traitor Sam Adams. He felt some sort of obligation to keep vilifying his role in the whole process, but in reality all the Barrister needed were results. Constant "explanations" or "justifications" were not desired at this juncture of the game. It was one thing to claim to be an informant, but it was entirely another to be that informant.

Yet this menace pounded on the window. He couldn't just do his assignment; instead, he sought counsel. And as the Barrister tried to enjoy his cigar, the passenger window of his sedan rattled with unexpected anticipation. Rolling his eyes and at last obligating himself to mortal duty, the Barrister rolled down the window.

"Yes?"

"I know where Shakespeare is."

This news shouldn't have been news but rather disclosure. Instead of berating the young bastard for his report, he decided to act upon it.

"And?"

"I need a team."

Sam Adams needed more than merely a team, but if he could prove successful in this mission, there would be high rewards for him.

"They've gone to Oak Island."

"That means nothing to me," the Barrister responded.

Adams walked away. The deal was made. A team would assert Adams's assumptions, and perhaps the villain would be captured. If not, the judgment of Christ would be forthcoming.

# NINETEEN

Oak Island was frigid at night. Far to the north and entirely too close to autumn, the outskirts of Nova Scotia were being hit by a heavy easterly wind from the ocean. Will had always preferred the Pacific. Its Latin name, *Mare Pacificum*, meant "peaceful sea." All along the West Coast, the Pacific lay like a slow-moving old man completely at peace with the world he lived in. Not the Atlantic. That was an angry ocean. Young and brash. Constantly bringing storms and struggle to the East Coast. It was such a small ocean, but it was so difficult to cross. So many lives had been lost. And here they stood, the first landing of European colonists and his Templar ancestors.

Prince Henry Sinclair knew the land was here, but what must his reaction have been upon seeing it for the first time? Meeting the Micmacs? It truly was the new Promised Land, the *New Atlantis*, as Francis Bacon wrote. New Jerusalem. The New World. It would be a world under secular law, far away from the whims of the Church. It would be a world bound by reason and science, built on hardworking principles and democracy. A radical new establishment run by the society the old world had tried to extinguish.

The Poor Fellow-Soldiers, and the Masons after them, had created the Americas as a haven for their kind. And centuries later, a revolution would create such a country. Now in the twentieth century, the Old World was still trying to destroy it. Those men in the church this morning were no threat. They kept secrets, yes, but only so that the knowledge wouldn't be destroyed or fall into reckless hands. They were not idealists or politicians. They were librarians and thinkers. To ignite such an age-old rivalry seemed ludicrous and cast light upon Sinclair's very purpose.

Henry Sinclair landed here and built one of the most elaborate hiding places the world had ever known. It was so ingenious, in fact, that after reading the documents, Will believed even if the island was completely gutted and taken apart, the modern world would still have no idea what secrets it held or why they were held there.

As they skirted a beach heading toward Smith's Cove, Will loosened up. They were now far away from the Money Pit, and any excavators would never hear their steps or voices, especially as the gentle waves caressed the shores around them.

"Are they digging up there?" Dorothy asked.

Being from Bermuda, it was very likely that she'd never heard of the legendary Oak Island and its mysterious secrets. They had a great deal of walking to do, so Will thought it a good idea to tell the story, partly to pass time, but also so she'd know what to expect as they went into Smith's Cove.

"They're probably drilling. That's called the 'Money Pit' up there. In the late nineteenth century, some boys discovered flagstones underneath a large oak tree. After digging underneath the stone, they realized they were digging in a man-made hole. Every few feet, they encountered a row of sealed oak platforms that they had to break through. Eventually they stopped digging. Another company, I believe it was Onslow, came in and started another hunt honestly believing it was the site of the treasure.

"They dug all the way through ninety feet, finding the oak layers every ten feet sealed with charcoal, coconut fiber, and putty. At ninety feet, they took a day's rest. It was the Sabbath. By the time they came back, the entire pit was flooded, and it remains that way to this day. Several treasure hunters have tried several other pits, including Franklin Roosevelt, but each time they try it, the pits flood. It was a booby trap set by Henry Sinclair in the late 14th century."

"You have got to be joking!" Dorothy said. "Who would have

the manpower or knowledge to set up something that elaborate in the 1300s?"

"You forget that Sinclair and his crew were Masons, exiled from Europe. They had building knowledge going back to ancient Egypt. These guys weren't amateurs. They built cathedrals! If anyone could build a system like this and still dupe modern science, it would be the Masons. And Sinclair ... well, he could be considered the father of the Masons."

"Why did the pits flood?"

"No one has cracked that puzzle. One clever gentleman put dye into the pit when he realized it changed with the tides. The dye turned up all around the island. As far as he could tell, the flooding came directly from the ocean on all sides.

"In 1850, they discovered the flood channel. What happened was, when they dug to a certain point, sealant was broken and the flood channels were opened, pouring the Atlantic into the pits. So, thinking they were clever, they put up a dam at the entrance to the flood channel. It didn't work, the ocean still got in."

"How?"

Suddenly Shakespeare stopped. Ironically, she'd asked that question just as they arrived at Smith's Cove. Kneeling for a moment, he dug his hand deep into the sand and found what he was looking for. Pulling fibers and grass from underneath the sand, he showed it to her.

"This sand was put on top of layers of coconut fiber and eel grass. It's essentially a massive sponge. This beach ensures that all of the cove's water will always get inside. Henry Sinclair built this beach. There's no way to block the water flow, not without completely blocking off the entire island."

She stood looking at him, stunned. For the first time since they met, she didn't furrow her brow when he said something. Instead, realization popped into her mind as she put the evidence together.

"Wait a minute," she said. "The treasure hunters know this?"

"Of course they do."

"Aren't you afraid they'll find out your secret?"

"They're looking in the wrong spot."

"The treasure isn't in the Money Pit?"

"The Money Pit is called that because millions have been sunk into trying to find out what's at the bottom. The thing is, there's nothing at the bottom at all."

She blinked and asked an inevitable question, "Then why the booby traps? The elaborate draining system? The sealed logs? A fake beach, for Christ's sake?"

He flinched at the blasphemy, but answered, "The Money Pit is only the first step to getting the treasure."

He stopped and looked into the sea. Turning back suddenly, he said, "Are you ready?"

"For what?"

"To take a swim."

# TWENTY

This man was crazy. What in the name of all that is good was Dorothy Wilkinson doing trudging around the extreme Northeast with a mad man? That wasn't even the full extent of the problem. She was seriously considering getting into the September chill of northeast Canada's waters to "treasure hunt" with an American loon. She was with an international traitor and likely a horrible kidnapper, and all she could do was nod and smile.

Standing on a beach, which was, apparently, constructed by one Henry Sinclair over 600 years prior, she had little choice but to play along despite her internal screaming objections. She was stuck now. Trapped in the world of William Shakespeare, either the world's most intelligent psychotic or the world's most necessary genius, she couldn't yet determine which. All she needed now, however, was assurance that her father and sister were safe. Suddenly the solemn coasts of Bermuda were but a distant and dangerous memory.

Sanctuary, hope, and security. After all she'd seen yesterday and today, could she honestly believe that Bermuda embodied such ideals? And what of her father? Was his illness only a ruse? Perhaps a way for her to understand her true calling? Was this man's conviction right? Were they holding the most important aspect of human history beneath their property? Was this far bigger than anything they pretended to be? Dorothy had already decided that anything found on her father's property belonged to her father, but what if she found what Shakespeare professed to exist? Could she honestly claim ownership over something so precious?

*What in the hell was the treasure anyway?*

Will Shakespeare was no help. Some obscure soldier in an even more obscure war. He spoke in riddles. This man, very well her captor, had done nothing but show cold sincerity. Without him, there was no passage to Bermuda, and with him there was chaos and lawlessness. At some point during their journey, she realized she'd have to settle with whatever Shakespeare had to offer. It was no longer under her realm of influence. This nonsense, perhaps instigated by a radical and lawless group, was being fed senselessly by Shakespeare's apparent lawlessness.

Now they were at some mystical place known as Oak Island— apparently the target of treasure hunters. Resigning herself to the whims of her captor, Dorothy followed him along the beach, listening to his account of the place. Not really acknowledging the full import of his knowledge, she simply looked at him in stunned silence when he told her they were about to go for a swim.

She didn't say anything; it could be perceived as weakness. Instead, she simply considered the prospect of diving into the ocean with nothing but her recently purchased business suit to protect her. It was too late now. She had to comply.

The sharp daggers of the Atlantic dove into her as she stepped into the surf. The water lapped insistently at her legs, and she shuddered as the chill overcame her body. Within a few steps, the water was already at her waist, caressing with painful fingers every available surface before she found herself chilled up to her chest. Will had gone in and ducked under, perhaps to adjust himself adequately to the extreme temperature. As he came back up, the water pulled back his hair in a display so striking she had to remind herself that this man could not necessarily be trusted.

Following suit, she lowered herself into the bay, allowing the salt water to envelope her body in a cold grip. It took only a moment, and she was acclimated. Suddenly things didn't seem so cold, and her suit, although ruined, was no longer a factor. Will dove under the water, and she joined him.

It seemed too long a distance to take a breath, but she saw his objective. Watching him underwater, she saw him disappear under a stone far beneath the surface. Below the stone was a much larger passage, and it seemed perfectly clear that she could resurface without a problem. Despite that, she felt compressed and out of breath. Swimming quickly behind her host, she hoped the surface would appear. At last it did. She let out a gasp and took in air that hadn't been breathed in many centuries.

# TWENTY-ONE

Distant headlights woke him up. Antoine wasn't accustomed to seeing headlights at Oak Island. It was still deemed private property, and his company was the only one with permission to be there. They'd paid handsomely for it. At first, he thought it could have been the police, perhaps taking a tour of the grounds, but then he recalled they weren't in the town of Chester's jurisdiction. The entire island was private. It had to be a tourist or, worse, a rogue treasure hunter. In either case, they wouldn't be treated kindly.

Antoine had fished out his pistol from his inside his tent and stepped pointedly onto the dewy ground. It was three-thirty, and none of the rest of the camp were awake yet. Rightfully so. He checked his ammo and pulled his trench coat tight, forcing out the harsh bite of the air. Squinting in the darkness, he could no longer see the headlights, but he knew the vehicle must have gone down the service road. It was the only road on the island.

The faint evidence of the headlights glistened from across the land bridge. Only streetlights were awake; the rest of the town was as asleep as his camp. Running his hand across a sandpaper chin, the French-Canadian hesitated before proceeding. The thought crossed his mind that they may be dangerous. A quick conclusion shut the thought down as he realized he had his gun with him.

He could wake the others, but there wasn't much point. He mostly wanted to scout them out and find out exactly what was going on.

If there was no need for alarm, he'd rather not wake the others. Just the previous afternoon he'd received a scolding from the camp leader about taking too many breaks, so he wasn't about to cause any more problems. If, on the other hand, he did capture some scavengers, he'd be able to take as many breaks as he wanted.

They'd been there three months and were no closer to making a discovery than anyone else that who had scoured Oak Island. The Money Pit was a ravaged trap of debris, mud, and water. The best they could do was drill and take core samples. They found some promising leads that prompted another pit fifty meters down, but, like the others, it had flooded. Just a week ago, they began exploring the flood tunnel that took in water from Smith's Cove. The four-meter-wide hole went straight into the island, bringing ocean water directly into the Money Pit. After exploring it thoroughly, the camp leader determined there was nothing new to be found and set his sights on other parts of the island.

Perhaps there was something after all. These thoughts occurred to Antoine only because as he stopped and quietly listened to the night air, he could most certainly hear voices coming from Smith's Cove. Young brown eyes looked into the night as he quietly moved forward.

He'd joined this operation against the will of his mother and father, who wanted him to join the forces and help rebuild Europe. He'd spent his life reading pirate stories, and when he heard another operation was being born on Oak Island, he jumped at the chance. They covered for food and lodging and paid a salary on top of that. Most importantly a small share of treasure would be awarded to all the workers. Antoine couldn't lose. It wasn't the treasure he'd come for though, he'd come mostly to see the legendary Oak Island with his own eyes.

Many sleepless nights were spent exploring the island after the camp shut down, and this night was no exception. It seemed as if fate had brought him there because only six hours ago, he was walking along the false beach of Smith's Cove, wondering what secrets the island held for its creator to put so much effort into keeping it hidden. Not even the best minds of the modern world had been able to crack this case.

The so-called breaks he was accused of taking weren't breaks at all. They were explorations, and if he found that one clue to solve this puzzle, the camp would feel sorry for scolding him so strongly. He was the youngest there and had a great deal to prove. Weak arms and stature made him poor at labor, and his cavalier attitude often came off as reckless.

If only he could find these perpetrators and prove his worth. Just then he saw a fully clothed couple descend into the bay. His brow furrowed as he realized they looked American. Quietly cursing under his breath, he put a foot into the water. Cursing again, he slowly went under.

# TWENTY-TWO

The air in the cavern whispered as soft, dripping echoes crystallized around them. Will couldn't see a thing. Reaching into his pocket, he pulled out his lighter, hoping the wick wasn't completely ruined and quietly cursing about having burned out the flash light on the way over. The cavern would have torches, but he'd have to find them without setting off traps. Dorothy's shimmering face lit up under his orange flame. Although her eyes were darting to all corners of the cavern, she didn't look scared. It seemed she took this sort of activity in stride.

The lighter cast delicate shadows on the cavern's walls. The ceiling was about twenty feet up, and stalactites hung with aged precision and in some cases came all the way down to the hidden harbor. Taking a survey of his surroundings, Will tried to recall what Sinclair's document said. It was less about discovering the correct path as it was about avoiding the wrong one. Stepping foot on the wrong shore of this cave could be very dangerous.

He treaded water for a moment and then noticed a darkened shadow off in the distance. Remembering a haphazard sketching in his mind, he figured that it must be where the staircase was. And where the stairs were, torches were. Light was the most important aspect of this part of the mission; without it, he could end up killing them both.

Gently taking Dorothy's hand under the water, he began back-kicking toward the crevasse. When they got near, Will saw steps ascending from the water up into a hand-carved hallway no bigger than six feet across and twelve feet high. This was the place.

They landed on the stairs and slowly walked up them without a word. Will ran his finger along the wall until he felt the expected shape of a torch. There were four more down in the hall and five on the opposite wall. They would just need one. He ran the lighter on top of the torch, and it immediately sparked into life. Even after six hundred years the torches worked. It was no wonder—handcrafted mahogany with a silver head and wick. They were built to last indefinitely.

Their scope of vision was much broader now, but not broad enough. The cavern took form around them. It was a semicircle encased in stone. Will knew that in the time of Prince Henry, this was merely a cove. They'd built walls up around and constructed a false beach above.

The trick was that this cavern was well under the water level. Will was astounded when he read the trap Prince Henry had built. The Money Pit was an ingenious way to drain the cave. It was dug farther than 200 feet down. Flood channels were constructed leading to this cavern and then beyond up to Smith's Cove. When the ninety-foot marker was breached, the flood channel was opened and this cavern was effectively drained into the Money Pit. It wasn't a booby trap at all but a key into the cavern. The only reason the cavern wasn't completely drained was because they stopped digging in the Money Pit. Had they gone deep enough, they'd be standing on the floor and not treading water.

The reason no one had found the cavern was because no one bothered to swim down the flood channel and up into the passageway that led to the cavern. Will wondered why the Poor Fellow-Soldiers never interrupted the treasure hunts, but assumed it was because they didn't want to arouse suspicion about the island by cutting it off.

Now they stood in the hallway where it had all begun. This was the holy of holies, where the treasure was kept. As Will lit the torch, he spotted another ingenious diversion across the cavern. Sitting protected in a niche were eleven sealed chests. Another chest on top of them was wide open, with an explosive pile of gold coins, statues, gemstones, and jewelry piled on all sides of the chests. It was a flood of brilliance, especially reflective under the torchlight.

The sound next to him was that of Dorothy losing her breath.

Then there was another sound far more serious than that. Will at once realized he'd left his gun in the car.

# TWENTY-THREE

Two black sedans careened down Highway 101 on the northern end of Nova Scotia. Driving the first one was Sam Adams. Nervously smoking a cigarette, he paid no mind to the other three men in the car. He had his platoon of soldiers. Eight fully armed men wearing suits and ties. They were deadly quiet, knowing full well the consequences of failure. The team leader would certainly be to blame.

Gnawing on the butt of his cigarette, Adams drove recklessly into the night. There would be no one on the road. It was only three-thirty. Fortunately, this time of year had yet to see frost on the road, otherwise their cars would skid out of control at this speed.

It was possible that he'd missed them, but not likely. He didn't know the particulars of Oak Island, only what Roland had disclosed at gunpoint. He needed only a few more minutes, and he'd capture the son of a bitch. Then it would all be over.

They passed the city limits of Chester. Oak Island was minutes away.

# TWENTY-FOUR

The sight was stunning. It was like nothing Dorothy could ever have imagined. The piles of gold and jewels were right out of a Robert Louis Stevenson book. Even from a distance and with only torchlight, the treasure was astounding. The pile reached several meters high with many unopened chests simply lying beneath it. There was unbelievably intricate gold dinnerware, crowns, jewelry … the list went on. The historical value of the treasure must have been priceless, let alone the monetary value.

Before she'd had a chance to fully take it all in, something horribly unexpected occurred. For the second time in as many days, a gun was pulled on her. Suddenly emerging from the cavern below was a young unshaven man wearing what appeared to be pajamas. He was holding a pistol rather aggressively and found stable ground to step on off to the side, opposite the treasure. Spitting the ocean water out of his mouth he looked frightened and looked between them and the treasure. Both parties were equidistant from it, but only he had a gun.

"*Qui êtes-vous?*"

Dorothy had no idea what he'd just said. The man looked to Will.

"*Les amis, ont mis le pistolet loin.*"

The young man scowled and looked at the treasure with such glee it was as if he'd encountered a lifetime obsession.

"American!" He spoke with a thick accent. "This is mine! Get away from it!"

"No! NO!" Will barked back. "Don't touch it, you'll kill us all!"

"*Ferme-la!*"

Will seemed very serious about this, and Dorothy wondered if he was playing him or if what he said was true.

"*Ne le touchez pas! Nous mourrons!*" Will shouted.

"*Dos loin!*" the young man commanded.

His mind was already made up. He was swimming for the treasure. Suddenly, Will grabbed Dorothy's hand so hard it hurt.

"I don't know who he is, but he'll kill us. The treasure is a trap."

Plans formulated across his face, and he only hesitated for a moment.

"Here," he handed her the torch. "Take this. Continue up these stairs until the hallway flattens out. At the end of the hall is a single chest. Open it. Inside is a box. Take the box, and whatever you do, *don't lose it.* Wait there for me. Don't go anywhere."

"Where are you going?"

"I have to stop him. Don't go anywhere. And *don't* lose the box. This whole thing was built to *protect that box.* If it's not the Holy Grail, it may as well be."

Will spun on his heels and dove into the water.

# TWENTY-FIVE

ntoine couldn't believe it. His heart stopped. After all this time. Hundreds of years, and it was he who'd found the Oak Island treasure. There it was, as easy as could be. He was the first. None of the bastards at the camp could ever have figured this out. He swam with all the strength he possessed. These Americans meant nothing to him. They were scavengers. Thieves. This was *his* reward.

As he swam he almost lost sight of them, but then their torchlight ascended into a nearby cavern. He couldn't see anything. Remembering that he had left his lighter back at the camp, he hesitated. It didn't matter. He wouldn't need it. The treasure was what was important. Pressing onward, now relieved that the Americans had left, he could sense himself growing nearer.

A black figure in the darkness jumped from out of the water and took him under.

*The bastards tricked me. This is my treasure! I earned it!*

He fought to regain buoyancy, but the attacker was too strong and kept him pinned under the saltwater. Flailing into convulsions, Antoine suddenly began to panic. He was going to drown without showing his discovery to anyone. This murderer was going to steal *his* treasure! All at once adrenaline pumped in again, and he tossed the attacker off, barely able to surface in time. Air filling his lungs once again, he looked around to orientate himself. His eyes had not yet adjusted, but a dim light from the torch in the chambers above glistened quietly off the gold. He was nearly there.

He was grabbed from behind in a tight hold. This attacker was very strong and skilled. He seemed almost militant.

"You fool," he said in mediocre French. "The gold is a trap. You'll kill us."

*Lies.* Antoine tried to wrench free but wasn't able to; the man's hold was too strong. Eyes starting to adjust, he saw something glisten slightly. It was a sword. A golden scimitar lying decoratively on the gold pile, and it was within reach. Lurching forward, he grabbed the sword and spun in the water, hammering the attacker square on the head. His grip was sloppy, however, and he smacked him with the broad side of the weapon, effectively smashing it in two. The attacker reeled back and fell into the water.

Antoine just then realized, to his horror, that the man was right.

# TWENTY-SIX

A flash of dull light reverberated through Will's brain as he was thwacked upside the head with a piece of treasure. Water overcame him, and he thought, or perhaps said out loud, that the end of the Templar legacy belonged to some French-Canadian treasure hunter. As he recovered and forced water out of his lungs by resurfacing, he heard the unmistakable sound of thousands of gallons of water pounding. Squinting in the darkness, now becoming acclimated with the help of the distant torchlight, he saw pillars of white water plunging into the cavern all around him.

*He sprung the trap.*

It was an ingenious trap, really, as most things that Prince Henry made were. The trap suggested that if anyone worth their salt knew that this was the location of his treasure, they'd also know where in the cavern it was. The documents disclosed a huge decoy that was set up exactly in the wrong place, and whatever scavenger came by would set it off. Touching the treasure broke another seal buried deep beneath the Money Pit, releasing all the water *back* into the chamber, effectively flushing out anyone inside before drowning them.

The broken seal also dropped the large boulder they'd just swam under, and after a reverberating thud echoed through the cavern, Will knew the trap had worked. There would be no way out. And as an added feature, it released another flood into the Money Pit from yet another channel. This ensured that the system was completely compromised and could never reveal its secrets to anyone. Smart thinking by the Templars ... if someone was close enough to set off the decoy, it was only a matter of time before they found the real treasure.

Even if they could make it back into the original flood tunnel and swim their way into the now-drained Money Pit, they would find it refilled just like before with another flush of water.

The water level was rapidly rising. It had already risen five feet before Will could recover, and judging by the faint shape of the steps that Dorothy had run up, they had only minutes before they were completely submerged. Ignoring the throbbing in his head, Will looked around for the idiot who'd set off the trap. Will found him cowering on the treasure like a wounded deer, hugging the world around him and watching his inevitable demise.

In other times, Will would have saved him, but it was far more important to get the real treasure to safety. Even though the civilian had hit him with a scimitar, Will couldn't really blame him. He didn't know any better.

*Shame.*

Leaving him cowering on the treasure, Will made his way back to the steps. As he did so, he went through his catalog of recently acquired knowledge about Oak Island. Surely Sinclair had left room for accidents. Perhaps he hadn't. Mental blueprints went through his mind, and they all came up with nothing. Pounding water sounded from behind, and he knew their time was short.

# TWENTY-SEVEN

The corridor was long and ancient. Dorothy's torchlight made ominous shadows on the walls like distorted demons crawling from the stone. Blackness radiated ahead of her, and no matter how bright her torch, it seemed to completely extinguish a meter ahead of her. Just when she was convinced she was going the wrong way, she saw an ornately carved chest at the end of the passageway reflecting her touch with gold-plated opulence.

Looking over her shoulder, convinced she'd stumbled upon another trap, she saw nothing but the darkness that was once ahead of her. A ridiculously loud pounding echoed from behind her, like a rushing waterfall crushing a riverbed. Whatever was going on back there wasn't good. Remembering Will's diligence, she proceeded to the chest.

It was unlocked, and that startled her. Again, looking over her shoulder for a trap, she hesitated before opening. Her breath was becoming short, and an ominous sense that she had very little time permeated every thought process. Quickly shoving aside any apprehension, she threw the chest open and quite anticlimactically discovered a tiny box inside, looking like it had just been thrown in as an afterthought.

The box had a familiar cross with wedged edges carved on it, and over that was the image of two medieval knights on a single horse. She'd seen that before in her studies and knew at once that it was a traditional Templar symbol. Will was right. It was all real.

The whole affair was completely legitimate. The realization rushed upon her like the crushing water in the cavern behind her. Her father held an ancient treasure on his property. She was the sole survivor of a Templar genocide along with the only person who preserved the secrets of the Order. It was now clear why he was so vocal about strange history ... he believed that he had to pass on the knowledge before it was completely gone.

She was learning things not even world leaders knew. She had in her hands the most valuable key in the history of human civilization. Her ... the sassy sprite from a British colony. What was her father wrapped up in? Who were the Masons really? So many questions poured into her mind, she almost forgot the purpose of the entire escapade.

She was seated, holding in her lap a small box retrieved from the treasure chest that Will described. Its heavy oak lid and rusty hinges made it difficult to open, but when she did, she was greeted with piles of silk around the sides of this small box. Inside was a small golden skeleton key. Believing it would be safer in her pocket than in the box, she slipped it in and buttoned her pocket. She then realized she could have bargaining power with all this. Closing and latching the box, she took that as well.

For the first time since they met, Dorothy was happy to see Will Shakespeare. Bleeding at the temple, he staggered into the hallway from below. The sounds of a hundred waterfalls echoed in from behind him. Before Will could say anything, a layer of water came up the hallway like surf, splashing unexpectedly onto Dorothy, who stood up, unable to stop a shriek from coming out.

"What the hell is going on?"

"He set off the trap. The chamber will be filled in a couple of minutes."

"Well, let's get out of here."

"No good. The trap dropped that boulder we swam under to get here."

"Where's the water coming from?"

"The Money Pit, but it's being filled by the beach on another cove."

It was silent for a moment, and she realized that the water was already at her ankles. Suddenly her heart fell, and coldness crept into the pit of her stomach.

"We're trapped?"

Will shrugged but didn't say anything. Looking at the rising water, he fell into a round of deep thought. Dorothy felt like panicking, but she knew it would be a waste of time. Still, anger rose up from the coldness in her stomach, and she began pacing. She didn't have to be here.

They both said nothing for long enough that the water was at their thighs. Suddenly Will's eyes perked up. He grabbed her hand and barked, "Come on!"

# TWENTY-EIGHT

A single thought put Will into a sprint back into the cavern. *The Money Pit had a decoy too.*

He'd managed to read the whole plan in between bouts of nausea on the car trip. In 1804, another tunnel had been dug extremely close to a decoy tunnel Sinclair's crew had built. An identical setup was created a bit farther out on the island to make it just that much more difficult to find the real treasure. It was only by chance that the real Money Pit was discovered first. When the other tunnel was dug, it flooded as well, but not because of this cavern. It was in fact an identical cavern that was drained. The other cavern had a decoy treasure and trap in at as well. Everything was the same except the key wasn't kept there.

A flood channel went between the two caverns to help flood the decoy cavern when the trap was released. It was the only way out. Will had absolutely no idea where the channel was except that it had to be low enough to drain into the lower decoy cavern. With only torchlight, it would be very difficult to spot. He tugged Dorothy into the water and headed toward the center of the cavern.

"Keep the torch lit, whatever you do. I have to find a way out."

"There is one?"

Just then, the young man swam over, panic illuminating his eyes.

"How do we get out of here?" Antoine asked, fear in his voice.

Will sighed and patiently pointed toward the corridor. "Go up there and grab a torch, I need more light."

With that, Will swam down. As he ducked under he noted that the water level was getting very close to the ceiling of the cavern. Currents of water poured around him from the jettisoning Money Pit. Feeling a bit out of control and wishing he'd spent more time swim training, he already felt his lungs under pressure. It couldn't have been more than a few seconds, but the currents were taking away his wind, and the brisk temperature of the water was numbing his fingertips.

At last he reached the floor of the cavern, but he saw nothing but blackness. Exasperation took his will to hold breath away, and he begun to resurface. Just then, another torch lit above and cast an orange pool close to the floor. Radiant light allowed him to squint and examine the surface.

Then he saw it.

# TWENTY-NINE

Dorothy took a mouthful of seawater as her head bumped against a stalactite. The water level was pushing her neckline, and just then the treasure hunter next to her lost his torch in the water. Keeping above water was becoming more and more difficult as the cavern ceiling pressed down upon him. She wanted to cuss out the companion next to her, but it would do no good, and she couldn't say she would have behaved any differently. Her complete lack of French stopped her communicating with him at all anyway.

It began to dawn on her that they may not get out of this. A cold feeling rose up in her stomach, and it wasn't the decreasing temperature of the chamber but the horror of realization. Casting thoughts around in her head, she had a difficult time settling on any one comforting place. Instead, panic rose, and she found herself pounding the ceiling of the cavern as the water level lapped against her chin. The French-Canadian fell beneath and gasped next to her, howling as he saw the air above him disappear.

Suddenly Will splashed out and crashed into the ceiling, apparently startled by how quickly it had filled. Spitting out water, he coughed for a moment.

"Gun," he gasped. "I need your gun." Shaking his head, he tried in French, "*J'ai besoin du pistolet.*"

The French-Canadian didn't hesitate. He passed the weapon to Will, his face pale and panicked. Dorothy felt a bit more at ease upon seeing him. She didn't know him well, but she saw a mission written across his face. He had calm blue eyes and a dedicated expression. He disappeared beneath the water, and for a moment they heard nothing. The moment turned into several, and now their heads were pinned at the ceiling, only their mouths and noses above the water.

Dorothy lost sight of the treasure hunter. Water consumed her, and she fought to keep it out of her lungs. The torch went out, and it was completely dark. Sloshing water and currents roared around her. Chills spun up her spine, and her breath began to fail.

*So this is it ...*

A blast echoed from beneath her, followed by a distant but profound creaking. Suddenly, the water dropped beneath her, and she was sucked under.

# THIRTY

His plan had worked, but he had no idea what the result would be. Under the dimming torchlight he'd discovered the flood chamber. Upon quick inspection, he saw a sealed layer of logs. Heavy kicks did nothing to budge it, so he surfaced to gather the only tool he had. Using a firearm under water had not, in any way, ever been recommended in his training. However, he knew it created a massive shockwave. Assuming he was lucky, the pressure wouldn't backfire on him.

He had to take the chance. With no way to brace himself, he took aim directly beneath him toward the flood chamber. Just then, the final torchlight went out.

*Guide my hand ...*

Trying to not change position, he closed his eyes and concentrated on his held breath. Pulling the trigger had created a huge and resounding boom. Currents whipped up around him and shoved him backward so suddenly it knocked the air out of him. Water began rushing into his mouth. Knowing he had less than three seconds before his lungs filled, he kicked violently upward. To his surprise, he found air. Vomiting water, he fought to stay afloat. Realizing at once he was alone in the darkness, he paused to gather his senses.

A sudden and unstoppable current dragged him back into the water, allowing him only a moment to take a burning and painful breath. His plan had worked. The chamber was open, and they were being sucked into the drain. There was no fighting this current. The vortex was taking in the entire chamber at thousands of gallons per second. Already pinned underneath, he had no choice but to hold his breath and wait.

In the next few moments, the world pounded around him. Having collided into the cavern floor, he was then sucked into even more darkness. Next was the extremely odd sensation of free falling. Although water was falling around him, he received a lungful of stale air. The moment was short-lived, and at once he was again underwater. He knew that they were very nearly in the exact same position as before, except this chamber had a way out.

Now above the rising water level, he looked around hopelessly in the darkness.

"Miss Wilkinson?"

There was nothing.

"DOROTHY!"

# THIRTY-ONE

It was a torrent of painful darkness. Tossed like laundry in a lightless abyss, Dorothy crashed into stone and felt the weight of the water around her suddenly release. It was enough time to get a lungful of air before she crashed into another subterranean lake. More saltwater. A waterfall pounded on top of her, and she found herself pinned underneath. Wrenched into flailing positions, she was, once again, running out of air. At last the pressure subsided enough that she could kick her way out, all the while gripping onto the small box. Swimming with nothing but adrenaline, she went as fast as possible. Her lungs felt heavy, and although panic was near, she knew the surface was close. To her horror, she crashed directly into the floor of the cavern, breaking off some stone and opening up cold gashes on her face and shoulder.

The air was gone and the pain drained her energy.

*The other direction.*

Renewed energy came from a deep and unknown place. Perhaps it was the will to live or the knowledge that her father would be in danger if she didn't return the key she held to Will—or maybe it was instinct. Whatever the case, she went into a frenzied swim, and just as her lungs were about to fail, she broke through the surface, gaping widely into the darkened and stale cavern around her.

A whisper in the darkness said, "Thank you, God."

She despised him for dragging her into this. She hated the situation her father had put them in. There was nothing about his knighthood she could respect. Kidnapping, guns, theft ... they were criminals. Yet when Will's firm hand gripped her shoulder and his arms brought her close to him, she felt safe for the first time since it all started. There was no one she trusted more. Instinctively she hugged him, grateful to be alive and thankful for the fact she wasn't alone.

He allowed the embrace for only a breath.

"Where's the treasure hunter?" he asked.

She had no idea. Looking into the dark cavern did little to help.

"*Bonjour! Êtes-vous là?*" Will barked into the blackness.

There was no response. Although sadness wafted over her, Dorothy was grateful to be alive. She knew it was a miracle she'd survived the fall. His safety wasn't their concern. Well, it shouldn't have been, but Will was persistent.

"Don't move," he whispered and then disappeared under the water.

*That man almost killed us!*

She suddenly felt very alone. The seawater was making her extremities numb, and the wounds on her head and shoulder were making her feel sick and faint. The cavern was completely silent, and there would be no adjusting to the light. There was no light to adjust to. Fear crept in, and to affirm it all she tried to see her hand and couldn't.

That was enough.

"Will!"

Nothing.

"SHAKESPEARE!"

Suddenly water exploded next to her, and his hand landed on her good shoulder. His weight took her down enough that she had to kick upward to stay afloat.

"I got him. It doesn't look good. Take my hand and do not let go," he said. "We are swimming down and through a passageway. We'll be right under the surface of a cove. Do you understand?"

Dorothy nodded and before she was ready, she was pulled under.

# THIRTY-TWO

It was exhausting. He gripped the unmoving and likely drowned civilian under one arm, and Dorothy's arm was clenched in his other hand. It occurred to him that, considering the circumstances, she was handling things quite well. All he had to swim with were his legs. Thankfully in the ocean, everyone was buoyant. He'd accidentally found the French-Canadian pinned under a stone at the bottom.

They were very nearly out because Will could see a sliver of midnight blue coming from the depths below. He didn't know exactly where it was, but based on the geography of the other cavern, it couldn't be far.

As they swam forward, the light grew more brilliant, even if it was still very dark. In the blackness of the cavern, however, the faintest light would seem extraordinarily bright. At last he could make out the shape of the underwater overhang. They were nearly there. They swam out from underneath, and although the water was the same, it felt much warmer and as broad and open as daylight. Without straining his breath, they surfaced. The first sight before him as he opened his eyes caused him to want to go back into the cavern.

There was no time. He ignored the looming silhouettes along the beach and brought the French-Canadian to the shore. Immediately landing the young man on his back, he searched his mouth for obstructions.

"Willy, how many civilians do you expect to bring into this thing?" one of the silhouettes asked him.

He was aware of Dorothy next to him, who, confused and worn out, collapsed onto the beach. Hoping to God that she still had the key, Will opted to answer the silhouette at a more appropriate time. The treasure hunter's face was void of all color, and his eyes were rolled back. He flipped the man over and raised his arms, then pressed on his back and elbows to push air through his lungs. There was no response.

"Leave it, Will. We have to talk," the persistent silhouette said under his breath.

Will ignored him, taking the civilian through another round. Doing some math in his head, he suspected the poor young man had been trapped underwater for at least three minutes. If only he'd brought him out sooner.

The distinct sound of a cocking gun echoed through the night, followed by a surprised grunt from Dorothy.

"Shakespeare!"

The voice was commanding, and it was only then that Will let it get to him. Stopping the procedure only once to look up at the threat, rage exploded from deep inside. This man was a traitor to thousands of years of history. A wormy translation of all that was bad in humanity. An insect. He'd taken Will's training and confidence and spat on it. He'd killed lifelong friends and destroyed an ancient institution. Now he was threatening Will's life as he was desperately trying to save another. It made no difference. Will had a mission. With or without Sam Adams' threats, he had to accomplish it.

"Shoot me, then," he said with unblinking coldness.

Returning to the task at hand, he went into another round of artificial resuscitation with the drowned man. Finally, he decided it was too late. There was no going back. Without equipment or professional assistance, this man could not be revived. The mission was over. Will rested momentarily and then stood to face Adams, who'd apparently decided not to follow through on his implied threat. Adams' eyes were stern but perhaps fearful. He held his pistol steadily, not as if to fire but to command. Six men stood behind him, nicely dressed and just as stern.

Will knew they were caught. There was no way out of this one. Stealing a glance toward Dorothy to see how she was holding up, he was relieved to see her eyes squinting with a glare, completely void of fear. Obviously, she'd seen enough to know who the bad guys were.

"You came for the key," Adams said plainly.

"We lost it."

"Bullshit!"

Adams forcefully pulled open Will's drenched and torn jacket to reveal an equally drenched and torn button-up shirt. Skillfully patting him down, he came up with nothing. There was nothing to find. Adams's hands then moved to Dorothy, and although it could have been considered invasive, there was nothing but professional coldness in his eyes. Spinning her around, he found the small box in the inside pocket of her suit jacket.

"Little souvenir?" he quipped.

Will knew what was next. Adams would destroy the key. At last, the Vatican would get its wish. The age-old secret would be annihilated in a storm, and the only key to save it would be gone forever. Not soon after, the only people who knew the secret would follow. The war was over. A soldier knew when he was defeated.

"Shall we take a little road trip?" Adams asked.

The others behind him broke poise only for an instant as they exchanged glances. This wasn't planned and was curious enough that Will tried to read their expressions further.

"Just get it over with, Adams. No need to drag this on."

"Get what over with? We're just getting started. Cuff them," he ordered.

Hesitant but obliging, one of the men stepped forward, producing handcuffs. Binding both of them behind their backs, he stepped behind them with a drawn weapon. They were now officially prisoners.

The Society of Jesus had no interest in taking prisoners or keeping artifacts. They wanted all the Templars dead, and they wanted their secret dead too. Adams was operating on his own. He wanted the Grail.

"Come on," Adams said as he turned on his heel. "We have a ways to go."

Within the hour, the prisoners were taken from Oak Island and left behind them the broken remains of a treasure that would never be found. The last person to know the truth was lying dead on the shore.

Quebec Countryside, Canada
September 9, 1947.

# THIRTY-THREE

It was a whirlwind, but Dorothy Wilkinson finally landed in a state of numb shock. It didn't do any good to dwell on the circumstances, figure out the implications, or in any way justify her situation. It was far better to experience each moment one after the next and allow the deep recesses of her mind to take in the damage. It was very nearly impossible to fully comprehend the past few days, and so she stopped trying.

Will Shakespeare was no help. Obviously a military man, he did nothing but recite information and provide his own version of the situation without offering any comfort or satisfying explanations. They were taken from Oak Island in a car before being deposited on a train leaving from Montreal. The militant zealots that captured them had enough influence to make the line's administration believe they were enemies of the state and were being transported back to Bermuda to be tried under international courts. This earned them a small car deep in the bowels of the train that had dim lighting, no windows, two cots, and a bathroom that was barely large enough to fit one person.

Will was very quiet for their two-day journey, and she hoped he'd spent that time finding a way to escape. She'd managed to get more information from him regarding their captors. The Society of Jesus was the secret military arm of the Vatican, though only those that had taken the superior oaths. They served one purpose: to protect the Church and to eliminate the Church's enemies. The secret knighthood was apparently top of their list, having since the 14th century, released the world from the Church's influence.

They'd done a fine job of eliminating the Templars, however the knighthood managed to blossom over the last 200 years despite that. And Masons took the virtues of the Templars and pushed them into society through world leaders, transforming the world into a democratic freedom-embracing one. This attack in Montreal, Will told her, was the first in hundreds of years and by far the most lethal. Although many Poor Fellow-Soldiers still existed worldwide, the entire leadership had been destroyed in that church. They were powerless and disbanded and would, one by one, disappear. He'd only hoped that the Masonic movement would be enough to carry the touch, maybe even perhaps the Masonic Knights Templar that embraced their oaths and tradition.

Will wouldn't speak of the treasure, not because he wasn't being forthcoming but because he had no idea what it was or why it was so valuable. Further discussion about that didn't come up again until that morning. Dorothy was feeling particularly bored and so forced conversation upon him.

"Why all of this nonsense over an antique cup?"

"It's not just that," Will explained. "The Holy Grail is far more than just a cup. It is far more than just a relic. It's a symbol. There are many stories about what it truly is, but I don't know which one is true. I'm convinced that the Catholic version is the most incorrect. They've always tried to hide the true nature of their history and their relics. The Church was built on a great deal of deception, and so to keep their integrity, they have to constantly reinvent history."

"What the hell are you talking about? The Church is built on deception?"

"You realize that the Catholic Church is a political institution, not a religion, don't you?"

Dorothy paused to indicate that she, in fact, did not.

Will sighed.

"Christianity is all well and good, but when you look at the Catholic Church as an entity, you must look at it as a political figure in history."

Dorothy's face was still blank.

Will ran his fingers through his hair and visibly collected his thoughts before proceeding.

"Let's start at the beginning," he said. "After the Crucifixion, Christ's apostles went forward and tried to spread his word. Mostly, they managed to put his teachings into script, and those became the first part of the New Testament. Do you follow?"

So far she did.

"It wasn't until Paul's time, much later, that the Christian Church spread and attained any influence worth mentioning. After a spiritual episode, Paul traveled the known world and established churches everywhere before he was finally crucified in Rome. Those churches, published in Paul's letters—the epistles—complete the New Testament, yes?"

It seemed like Sunday school stuff, but yes, she remembered. Nodding, she asked him to continue.

"Paul is credited with establishing the Catholic Church, which means roughly the 'universal church.' His church is considered to be a bit different than Jesus' teachings, particularly in certain dogmas and rituals. But I digress. His influence was profound enough to spread Christianity to the masses so much that the Roman Empire was threatened. They did a great deal of persecution of this 'cult,' hoping that the monotheism craze wouldn't spread.

"It did, and did so dramatically. In fact, a Roman emperor, Constantine, converted to Christianity, and that was the start of the Roman Catholic Church. This institution was a political move by Constantine. He saw a great deal of potential in creating a government based on religion and not on politics. His conversion of the Roman Empire was legendary and created the paradigm from which the Catholic Church operates today.

"Before he could establish such a church, however, he had to establish some ground rules. This is why I say the Catholic Church was based on deception. In the Council of Nicaea, Constantine and prominent Church leaders established arbitrary rules that strayed heavily from Jesus' teachings.

"By the time Pope Urban II was in office, these rules were not only the spiritual paradigm, they were the actual rules of kingdoms in Europe. The Crusades were a way for Pope Urban II to turn a spiritual agenda political and create a military force around the Church. The Templars were certainly a part of that, as was the Order of Malta and many others."

Dorothy paused, hoping his lecture would sink in. After a while, she sighed.

"You have a lot of strong opinions regarding history. I can't help but think you're making the whole thing up."

"There's a lot to know," he said. "And it's never taught. I'm only giving you sketches of the real story. I'm abbreviating because no one wants to hear that the entire world they know is wrong. The truth is very painful."

"I'm Anglican; you have yet to insult me."

"Wait long enough," he quipped.

They both indulged in a chuckle, and as Will straightened up, he took her hand.

"You're very brave," he said. "I wouldn't have forced this experience on anyone."

"I haven't got a choice," she said.

"There is a way out."

"I believe you."

The 'poor knight' picture began making a bit of sense. For the first time, she started accepting that perhaps it was a legitimate organization. Will certainly believed it was, and after these few days with him, she was inclined to believe it too. He was a man with solid convictions and enough evidence, though strange, to support them.

"So, tell me about the Holy Grail."

He sighed. "That is a long story."

"Isn't it the whole point of the Templars?"

"That's also a very long story."

"Stop saying that, Sir Shakespeare. We have time," she said, her annoyance beginning to show.

Will reached into his ocean-worn pocket and pulled out one of the few remaining cigarettes he'd managed to get from Adams. Taking a puff, he passed it on to her. Grateful to have it, she took the cigarette and waited for Will to continue.

"During the Crusades, the Templars incurred a lot of wealth from the primary antagonists—the Saracens. You see, Pope Urban wanted to retake Jerusalem in the name of Christianity, and that we did, after a very bloody battle. We were given strict access to the historical relics of Jerusalem, but no one could have guessed what we actually found.

"Caliph Omar, one of the most notorious Arab leaders, stashed a great deal of his most precious items in Jerusalem. After he sacked the Library of Alexandria in 640, he took its holdings there. Most think that the knowledge of the Great Library was lost, but it wasn't."

"That's the treasure? A bunch of books?"

Will shrugged. "No one knows what exactly it is. Books, sure ... well, scrolls and parchments. But it's the content of these books that has the world guessing. The only men who knew anything at all about that were killed three days ago."

Quick to change the subject, he continued, "The Templars kept the secret very close all the way up until the fourteenth century. Most of the artifacts were kept in France, where the knighthood was primarily located. After an angry mob chased him, Phillip IV took refuge with the Templars. Somehow, he discovered our secret and immediately saw us as a threat to the Church. There was one thing in particular Phillip, and Pope Urban through him, wanted."

He paused to steal a drag off the cigarette.

"A map."

"A map?"

"We had, in our possession, the *Mappa Mundi*. It was an accurate and detailed map of the world. The whole world, I mean. The Americas and everything down to the Andes Mountains and the Gulf of California."

*Unbelievable. He's going there again.*

"What do you have against Christopher Columbus?"

"Nothing," Will said plainly. "But he took a great deal of credit for something he didn't do. Modern historians say that Columbus was born Cristoforo Colombo in Genoa. Actually, he was Cristobal Colon, born in a Jewish ghetto in Genova. He was the illegitimate son of Charles IV. A crewmember for René d'Anjou, sailing with the best of them at age twelve. By twenty-five he'd navigated all over the Mediterranean and as far as Africa. He fell into favor with Spain's royalty, and the rest is history. Colombo's history wasn't as dramatic. He bought and sold wool in the Greek Islands and later got into the sugar trade out of Portugal. Columbus couldn't even speak Italian. He spoke Spanish.

"So this map, this *Mappa Mundi* ... who in the hell would know about the whole world at that time?"

"That's the real question, isn't it?" Will sparked. "And the answer is the Holy Grail."

"A cup?"

"No, a symbol of the most valuable knowledge in human history. We call this secret knowledge the 'Holy Grail.'"

"Why are you telling me all this then if it's so secret?"

He paused, apparently struggling with the answer. After stealing another hit from her cigarette and returning it to her, he said, "If I die, many of the secrets die too."

Will was actually handing the weight of his society's responsibility to her. Why she was the one who got the burden she didn't know. And in fact, she wasn't sure she could remember all this. She wasn't totally convinced he was speaking the truth. Perhaps this ancient knowledge was a series of parables and false history just to keep people guessing. But ... a map of the world before Columbus?

"This map," she said, wanting to get away from the prickly subject, "this is what the Church wanted?"

"Absolutely, and so did Phillip and all the other Church-loyalist monarchs. On a day that's now popularly called Friday the thirteenth, the Church and Phillip rounded up all the Templars they could find in Europe and tortured them to find the location of the map. The Templars were charged with heresy, and eventually they were all killed. Although they confessed to heresy, they never disclosed the real location of the map."

"Where was it?"

"Scotland. They sought sanctuary with Robert the Bruce. Years later, Prince Henry Sinclair took a fleet to Nova Scotia and buried the treasure there. The rest you know."

"Not quite."

Will raised an eyebrow at her.

"We found a key in there, not a treasure," she said.

Will nodded and then took a breath.

"Sinclair's document told me something I didn't know. That I suspect only the men in that church knew. The treasure was moved."

"Moved? From where?"

"From Oak Island. The Templar treasure was moved when the French colonials came in. The Templars moved it."

"Where?"

"Bermuda," he said quietly.

She glared at him. It was all she could do to avoid falling apart. *The Holy Grail is on my property? The Holy Grail? IN BERMUDA?*

"Will," she said in a dry tone, "you're telling me that the Templars moved the Holy Grail from Canada ... to Bermuda."

He nodded somewhat meekly.

"Sounds a little ridiculous to me," she said. "Who moved it? Surely it would have been one hell of a navigator."

Will shrugged and said, "Francis Bacon."

She happened to know quite a bit about Sir Francis Bacon, having had a colonial education. In fact, her tutor, Miss Taylor, had demanded that she write an essay on the philosopher in secondary school. It was a good one and earned her a high mark. The possibility that Bacon, as prolific and educated as he was, was involved in a global crusader plot to move the Holy Grail from Canada to Bermuda was not only laughable but insulting.

What Will told her after her next inquiry, however, could not just be passed off.

"How did Francis Bacon know the treasure was here?" she asked.

"Francis Bacon knew the treasure was here because his father was one of the Poor Fellow-Soldiers' most prominent figures of the time."

Her brow furrowed as she visibly tried to recollect Bacon's father.

"The history books will tell you differently, but Francis Bacon was the son of Sir Francis Drake and Queen Elizabeth the First."

"Now you've gone too far," she barked. "It's one thing to insult the Italians by suggesting that Columbus didn't discover America ..."

"Columbus wasn't Italian."

"But now you're saying that one of the world's most famous explorers and one of England's most popular queens gave birth to English philosopher Francis Bacon, who set sail on the seven bloody seas to move some ancient bleeding treasure buried in Canada to my father's property?"

"Francis Bacon did just that, as per the instructions of his father."

"That's it. You will not hear another question out of me!" she said, crossing her arms over her chest, a scowl on her face.

"Drake began the transition shortly before his untimely death during a spat with the Spanish," continued Will. "Bacon had no choice but to continue the effort. It took him several years, but at last he finished and sealed the deal by taking territories in Newfoundland to make sure no one picked up on the trail."

"And it's still there."

"Your family has been in the Order's good graces. I read contracts going back generations in that file. When the Wilkinsons discovered the Crystal Cave in 1884, the Poor Fellow-Soldiers were left with a terrible choice. Not wanting to needlessly spill blood, we decided to negotiate with your family. For a moderate sum, they promised not to go into certain parts, and we simply kept an eye on it all. It wasn't a problem until recently, when the war brought so much military activity. We asked your father to close the caves to the public. He agreed without question."

She'd always wondered why he'd done that. It seemed a waste of potential income after the rise of tourism since the war. The payments he received or his relationship with those men must have somehow outweighed what he could have made from the tourists.

Then again ...

"My father is not a poor ... whatever ... soldier!"

"He's a Mason, and that's enough. Masons are extensions of our Order. Many of our squires are prominent Masons, even if they have not taken oaths, been trained, or initiated into the secret world."

If a higher-ranking Mason told him to shut the caves down, he would have, Dorothy thought. He was an avid Mason and took great pride in it, although he never spoke of the particulars. She suddenly missed him very much. It had been a while since she'd seen him, and after all that had happened, she wanted nothing more than to be home. Being held on a train in Canada didn't make her feel close to home; in fact, she might never return. She was stuck in this tiny cabin with a soldier from some secret society.

They'd fallen into silence again. That was enough for now. It had all been almost too much to absorb.

New York City, New York
September 10, 1947.

# THIRTY-FOUR

Will found himself pacing. Ever since their capture, he'd been working on a plan that seemed impossible but at the same time was necessary. If no one knew the secrets the Poor Fellow-Soldiers kept sacred, then thousands of years of history would be nullified. He couldn't be the one that let the Catholic Church determine true history. The integrity of his knighthood and the success of the human race depended on his vigilance in his mission. This one could not fail. Despite the odds and the circumstances, in this case, he had to be right. Even if he couldn't make it, he had to do it for Dorothy's sake. He'd disclosed enough secrets for the truth to move on without his help. She may not believe him or have the whole story, but she knew enough to keep the legacy alive and to ensure its history would be portrayed accurately despite how religious organizations would corrupt it.

Despite his constant thought process, he could think of nothing to help them escape. In fact, the entire scenario seemed well beyond the bounds of sense. The Catholic Church had no interest in preserving true knowledge or seeking Templar treasures. Those days were long gone. The Catholic Church was on a very progressive path of trying to integrate with world politics and was fundamentally supporting their spiritual positions. Pope Pius XII wouldn't be interested in an age-old grudge and, more importantly, wouldn't be interested in the wealth the grudge would hold. To suggest the Jesuits were in any way commissioned by the current pope would be ludicrous. Even Will knew they had to be operating on their own.

The Society of Jesus took Templar triumph far harder than the Vatican ever did. Although it was possible that politics were involved, Will was smart enough to know that was unlikely. This was a far more thorough and aggressive plot. The fact that Will and Dorothy remained alive was evidence that these men were acting on their own. They were after the treasure, not the ideal. If Pope Pius were in charge, Will and Dorothy would be dead by now. Instead, they were leading their captors to the treasure. They'd be the key because those in control had no concept of what they were dealing with.

They weren't members of the secret world. If they were, they'd realize the full extent of what they asked. Will Shakespeare would not turn over his secrets to them. There was only one person he trusted, and she was a civilian. Shoving thoughts of the treachery aside, he had more important things to consider. Their escape.

Most importantly, they had to recapture the key. Any escape would be pointless without it. A plan had been brewing in Will's subconscious. Watching very carefully how they were treated, Will knew they were under strict supervision, but he also knew their captors underestimated their position. His plan had to be launched at just the right time, during a window of opportunity when they wouldn't be noticed, while at the same time utilizing the train's location. It would be no use to escape into wilderness, and likewise, escaping only to be trapped on the train was equally pointless.

His attempt to figure out their location was perhaps weak, but it was as close as they were going to get. Assuming the train was moving at a standard speed, it was heading for the United States, and he suspected they were very close by now. Within two hours, they'd be stopping at New York, and the plan would have to be executed before then. Although Adams was less trained than Will and was completely unsuspecting of Will's plan, he was still a dangerous foe. With other highly trained comrades in the Society of Jesus, Will wasn't only outmatched but also outwitted. Most of these adversaries had far more knowledge than he did.

He cringed to think Adams was a traitor. Franklin had handpicked the little bastard, and that man was hardly ever wrong. Suddenly, Will found himself thinking about Franklin, and a wave of melancholy overcame him. He slowed his pace and leaned against the wall as Dorothy tried to amuse herself by picking at her nails. Franklin was his friend and mentor. Shaking stray thoughts away, he remembered he was still on a mission. Once they were out of this, he'd have plenty of time to wrap his mind around this whole thing. Right now, he had only one objective.

Perhaps they were in third class so the captors could keep their prisoners close. It then occurred to him that Adams could be anywhere. It was a suicide mission to hunt down the key. His ideas ran away from him. The weight of the last few days, his exhaustion and hunger were all impairing his judgment. He'd never have considered this plan under normal circumstances. Nervous energy sprang up from inside his stomach, and he felt, for a moment, petrified.

*They could just go.*

He needed the key. But at what cost? What good was the key without Dorothy's directions? Couldn't he find the treasure without her? Master and Commander Franklin was very specific. He said to make sure she lived. As a soldier, he was not to question the motive, but now he needed to know if it was her knowledge about the storm that was important or something more. There was no time to speculate. He had to assume she was as precious as the treasure. Besides, after all they'd been through in the past couple of days, he couldn't simply abandon her.

He was only projecting. There was no telling what Franklin meant by his order, but it was an order. Even if the Holy Grail was lost forever, his mission was not to find it. His mission was to make sure Miss Wilkinson lived. Those had been Franklin's words. Will finally rejected anything contrary to that. Putting the treasure out of his mind, he began thinking about how to get off the train.

Then the moment Will was waiting for happened. The steady and slight tremor under his feet changed, and the engines suddenly lowered their tone into a semi-detectable baritone. They were slowing down. As he whipped out his lighter, Dorothy suddenly looked up.

"You have cigarettes?" she asked like a child on Christmas.

He shook his head, not explaining. The previous night he'd

prayed that they'd get more cigarettes. The empty prayer had yet to be answered. Instead, he spent his time chewing on his teeth. A dedicated soldier barely noticed such a small thing.

The lighter still worked, and that was all he could hope for.

"Miss Wilkinson ..."

"Will, I think we've been through enough. You can call me 'Dorothy.'"

It wouldn't be chivalrous. The mission would have to be over before he ever called her that. He remembered a moment  in the cavern when he'd called her by her first name. It didn't matter—that had been a time of duress. This wasn't, although it could turn into one.

"I'm leaving you, but only for a few minutes. I don't want you to get upset or in any way bothered by this."

Her wide eyes went wider.

"You're leaving? This cabin? And just where are you going? Cocktails?"

"We need clothes."

She laughed, assuming it was a joke. It wasn't. That was integral to his plan.

"Don't come after me, and if someone comes while I'm gone, don't do anything stupid."

"Like what?"

"Like telling them what I'm doing."

"How could I do that? I haven't the foggiest idea what you are doing."

"I told you," he said. "I'm going to get clothes."

As if he had a key to the train car door, he twirled around and faced it. In a way, he did have a key. Will had known all along how to get out of the car the moment he was put inside it. A few seconds under flame would cause the cheap aluminum latch to buckle. As he put his theory into practice, the door obliged and the handle popped up.

Will didn't fling the door open and make a run for it; that would have been reckless. Instead, he quietly peeked out, and then, before leaving, he gave Dorothy a brief reassuring smile. It meant only that he'd be back.

"Don't forget to write," she said.

Snorting a laugh, he proceeded carefully into the train.

# THIRTY-FIVE

Flabbergasted that the only person she trusted was now leaving her, Dorothy stared back at him with wide, unblinking eyes. His smile passed over genuine affection to her and softened the blow. Could this secret soldier actually admire her? Probably not. In any case, it wasn't the proper time to consider such things. After all, they'd only just met and were at the moment captured on a train by fundamentalist Catholic warriors bent on destroying world history.

She was growing accustomed to the lifestyle. Although jarring at first, regular use of firearms, vigilance, and murder were becoming everyday activities. Before long, she'd be creeping down corridors with pistols, barking orders at someone. It would be very difficult going back to a regular life now ... if she ever made it back.

The notion that this might be it for her had crossed her mind more than once in the past couple of days. Even now she saw no way out of their current predicament. Blind trust in an eccentric stranger was never a good and stable path to safety. In fact, she'd done everything wrong. All those instinctive things and even the things she'd learned had been violated from the very start. The only way through was to numb herself, and she'd done such a good job of that she'd hardly felt a spark of emotion since the cavern.

Thoughts of Oak Island sent her mind to Bermuda. She wondered how her father and sister were doing. They'd expected her back by now and would surely be worried about the imminent approach of the hurricane. Probably already stocked up, her father would have put the supplies in their waterproof shelter beneath the house. They'd spent many a hurricane season down there, listening to the radio and harboring other Bermudans who were less fortunate. Although the swells were certainly a concern—one bad season the shelter was actually submerged for three days—her father had built the shelter mainly for hurricane-induced tornadoes. In a small island home, they stood no chance against winds that strong and barely a chance against standard hurricane winds. Her father's house had stood up to 100-mile-an-hour winds before, but this hurricane would certainly challenge that.

She knew that if they didn't get back within five days, the winds would be too strong to return there at all. Even if they left from New York the next day, it would take three days to reach Bermuda. They couldn't handle very many more delays. Once the storm hit, whatever it was Will needed would be forever lost, and she wouldn't be able to return home for at least a couple more weeks. And if it was, in fact, the Holy Grail ... then ...

Dorothy was idly reflecting on Bermuda when the door flung open with such fervor she leapt back into the corner of the cabin.

# THIRTY-SIX

The Atlantic gently lapped waves onto the man-made beach of Oak Island. The Barrister gripped his bald head with frustration. Looking out over the rising Atlantic sun, he twirled his pistol subconsciously with his free hand. A sideward glance at three of his ministers suggested he was ready for them to come forward.

"My dear mother once told me," he said to the ministers, "never trust a hound that sleeps with the fowl. Gentlemen, we've been duped."

His Liverpool accent was thick with disdain. Pivoting to face them, he continued, "If we are to ensure that the heretic history of man will never rear its ugly face again, we have to know for certain that every last Poor Knight is dead after this storm destroys their secrets. These men are grotesque insults to God's creation and Christ's message. Paganism, lies, sodomy, idol worship ... the list goes on. At last, the crusade is coming to a close, and some poofter ... some bleeding, mindless git, saddles up his bloody horse and goes on a bleeding treasure hunt! AND YOU WENT WITH HIM!"

The twirling pistol in his hand settled, and with a single gesture he shot one of the men between the eyes. The other two didn't flinch or even falter. They kept placid expressions and continued to look at their rector.

"I should shoot the lot of you," he said under his breath, "but I won't. There are still four more of your men on a train heading to New York. Where are they heading?"

One man answered in a rehearsed military tone, "Adams knows the treasure is in Bermuda, but he needs the hostages to tell him exactly where. Using some contacts in the American military, he is going to take an aircraft to Havana and then take a boat to Bermuda."

"Why aren't you with them?"

"We decided that Adams must be behaving outside your orders, so we mutually decided to dispatch ourselves in order to confirm it, sir."

Confusion crossed the Barrister's face as he reviewed the impulsive murder he'd just committed. Without wavering, however, he simply said, "I see."

Pausing, he turned to look at the sunrise. A golden plateau of clouds stretched across the flat expanse ahead of him. He knew that all the triggers in Oak Island were set, and no matter where anyone dug, they'd reach more water. The secrets here were buried forever. Now they had to rid themselves of the Templars and their biggest secret north of the Caribbean.

"We cannot reach New York in time, so we must intercept them in Havana. Our ship is waiting. Before you gather your things, make sure this camp of treasure hunters is disassembled."

"And the people here, sir?"

"You heard me," he answered coolly.

The implication was clear, and they left to clean the island, leaving their fallen comrade alone and dead on the beach next to the drowned civilian.

His murder wasn't justified. The Barrister whispered a Hail Mary under his breath as he pulled a knife for his penance.

# THIRTY-SEVEN

There were two policemen standing outside, and they hardly had time to react to Will when he snuck out. Knowing full well their training was nowhere close to his, he easily overcame them with five gestures. He grabbed one pistol from the policeman's holster, whipped the other one into unconsciousness, gestured for the first one to get on the ground, and then he cuffed them both.

Now that he was outside the train car, it was clear where they were. The oncoming display of skyscrapers meant only one thing. He blinked, suddenly stunned as he saw the famed Chrysler Building. It was almost twenty years old, but he remembered it going up. The critics at the time were quite right: it was a monstrosity. Defying the standard skyline with obstinate architectural betrayal, it permanently glared upward. Margaret Bourke-White had done a clever job of masking its protrusion in her famous photograph.

Distractions aside, he regained his composure and walked carefully into the next car. Knowing full well he would stick out far worse than the Chrysler Building, he peered inside before venturing forward. Still wearing torn and soiled clothing from Oak Island, he'd long ago abandoned his tie and lost his second hat of the week. Only a ruffled suit coat remained, which had been given to Dorothy the moment they stopped to dry. He was left with a shirt missing over half its buttons and slacks torn at the hem. He hadn't shaved in three days, and the subtle scruff on his face and neck was blossoming into a beard. Unkempt and tousled hair strayed aimlessly over his eyes. Apart from his appearance, he was terribly hungry and had had only the smallest amounts of water. Energy was far removed, and without the aid of sleep, he had a blank and baggy expression etched on his face.

The next car was for luggage and passenger cargo. The lights were off, and it made sense that they'd been put in a similar car. Chances were that there was another car full of this stuff. A black sedan took most of the space, and Will decided that must belong to his captors. Luggage was piled up around it, and a large birdcage with an exotically colored parrot loomed over the sedan. It didn't much matter what the other cars held because his objective was far closer than he'd originally thought. Will opened up the first suitcase he found. Inside was a woman's suit, but it was far too big for Dorothy. He kept looking and at last found suits that would fit both of them. After another round of looking through hatboxes, he found a replacement gray fedora and a petite hat with netting for Dorothy. Another travel case revealed a razor, soap, and other sundries. Dumping it all into a single suitcase, Will suddenly realized that the train was slowing.

Not missing a beat, he charged through the door and back into their car. The policeman was regaining consciousness, but both men were still cuffed. Leaping over them, Will crashed into the room.

"We have to go. Now!"

Startled but quick to act, Dorothy jumped to her feet and joined him outside the car. She stood, also stunned, looking at the city around her. They'd traveled quite a distance since Will had last looked out the window, and so before Dorothy could comment, he dragged her by the hand into the cargo car. Handing her the suitcase, he said, "Hold this. Don't move."

"You act as if I'm some stupid child who strays in shops."

He paused for a moment and, instead of responding, opened the car door again. They'd soon be at Grand Central, and he was ill prepared for an escape. They had to get off this train before then. Surely the police would already be rounded up. There was only one way he could think of to get away.

Lifting the connecting platform, Will saw the coupler below swarmed in hoses and wires. A sideward glance revealed the location of the cut lever, and he reached over with a minor grunt. Without leverage on his reach, he couldn't make it budge. He crawled onto the car's ledge, gripping the opened door. Dorothy watched him with a furrowed brow. Ignoring her, he proceeded to the edge, where he could see the city streets passing at forty-five miles per hour. He kicked the cut lever, but it still didn't budge. Realizing it was probably locked for safety, he carefully crouched to inspect it more closely.

There was a latch at the bottom of the lever that had presumably been put in place before the train left. He released the latch and pressed the lever down. The couplers opened, but the cars were still connected. At first he thought it was the wiring and hoses that kept it together, but then he noticed the coupler pin. Crawling back to his original position, he took a strong foothold inside the cabin and reached out from the open door, pulling the pin out. The cars were still attached, and this time it was indeed because of the wires and hoses. Unplugging the wires left only the hoses to keep the cars together, but that wouldn't last long. Will closed the door and watched as they ruptured.

It took only a few seconds. Water, steam, and air whipped out from the hoses as the car detached and fell backward. His plan had worked; now they were in the last car. The train had slowed when it reached the city limits, and Will estimated that they only had a few minutes left before they rolled into the station. At that point, his plan would no longer be viable. Quickly clearing out a path between the sedan and the rear of the car, he turned to look at a confused Dorothy.

"You ready to go?" he asked.

# THIRTY-EIGHT

Cherry pipe tobacco filled his mouth, and he fought the urge to inhale. *Only savor the flavor and let it out*, he mused. Reclined on a very comfortable seat, Adams allowed himself a scotch as they entered the city. New York's skyline loomed above a thick morning fog. The streets were already cluttered with cars and workers. The skyline was close; they would soon be in Manhattan, minutes from Grand Central Station. Sipping the scotch brought him comfort, briefly anyway. More than he'd received in quite some time.

Glancing over at the men, he offered a grin.

"Almost there, gentlemen."

They were not amused.

"The Barrister put me in charge. These are his orders. What else do you want from me?"

One man looked away, but another maintained his cold stare.

"If this is true, then you have nothing to be nervous about."

"Why wouldn't it be true?" Adams smiled, but inside his nerves jumped.

He knew full well that he'd stolen the men from the Barrister, and he'd be hunted down for this, but he needed them, and he had better protection with them around—more effective than even the Vatican. The man he answered to could destroy these men with a single thought. They were only tools to reach the most valuable treasure in the history of man. With that power in his hands, even the Jesuits would shine his shoes at his request.

His nerves softened as he thought about his future. They wouldn't be soft for long. One of the men jumped to his feet to look out the window. Adams thought his name was Christopher or one of the other saints. Hell, they were all named after saints except for the Barrister, who kept his secular nickname for intimidation.

"God help us," he said.

Although his nerves were heightened, Adams didn't want to know what Christopher had seen. Nevertheless, he casually leaned forward and took a look out the window. All composure suddenly crashed, and Adams dropped his pipe as he lurched to his feet. The last car of the train was sitting stationary on the tracks, far behind the moving train.

Without a word, he pulled out his pistol and bolted for the door. A cleverer member of his party immediately jumped up and pulled the emergency brake on the train. Horrific screeching bounded through the air as the occupants of the car tumbled onto each other. The surrounding city stopped to look. Many cars pulled over, passengers stepping out to see what the emergency was, and passersby ran up to the rail.

After he regained balance, Adams nearly lost it again. The train was curved enough on the track to allow them a very clear view of the last car. The back of the train had just exploded from the impact of a sedan parked inside. The sedan crashed onto the rail and squealed off into the city.

"DAMN IT!" Adams barked and squeezed his way off the passenger car in search of his own vehicle.

It was the last time he'd underestimate Will Shakespeare.

# THIRTY-NINE

She was now a criminal working for an unknown organization breaking international laws and violating treaties—a refugee from Bermuda crossing the border after escaping and eluding Canadian authorities. Guilt overcome with anxiety decorated with panic took over her consciousness. Asking herself once more what she was doing, she could barely hear herself over her mental scream. The mental scream turned physical as Will Shakespeare drove a car off a train. Tumbling forward in a pile of jerking momentum, she managed to miss the dash only barely with help from a lap belt.

The broken, bleeding man beside her—a few days ago a stranger—recovered from hitting his head on the steering wheel. Apparently, it was only a flesh wound because he pushed forward while alertly glancing in the rearview mirror. The street tried the sedan's resistance and the accuracy of the steering wheel. The proximity of the storefronts to the street threw human obstacles in the way. The small urban roads fell into geometrical chaos, every couple of blocks introducing traffic, diagonal intersections, and ninety-degree turns.

After Will took several wild turns in the depths of Harlem, Dorothy checked the mirror. She saw only the wrecked chaos of the turns behind her—toppled bread stands, screaming vendors, startled businessmen, and activated policemen. She didn't see anyone pursuing them.

"I didn't sign up for this," she said to Shakespeare.

"You didn't sign anything."

As attractive as Will could be, with his calm clarity and rawness, the same qualities made her furious at times. She glared over at him.

"Then why am I here?"

"I'm keeping you safe."

"This is safe?"

"Would you rather be back on the train?" he asked as they came upon another intersection.

The turn was tight, and in a few moments, they were bumping down a torn street called Fort Washington Avenue. They passed Broadway and a once-beautiful park with benches and a pond, but poverty had turned it into a wasteland of squatters. The high-rise apartments on the other side of the street toward the river were obvious victims of poverty and crime. Only the remains of their scaffolding held up some buildings, completely abandoned.

St. Nicholas was a straighter street than the last, but it was far more congested. Will had a difficult time keeping the car in line. Every few seconds they'd jerk to the side because of a sudden swerve or unexpected obstacle.

She checked the rearview again. What were they running from?

Just as she looked forward again, her heart jumped and an immediate surge of adrenaline brought sweat to her brow. A black sedan had just come from 153rd Street. With the narrow buildings and oddly configured streets, they might never have seen it.

Will immediately turned the car right onto a diagonal street, Convent Avenue, that burrowed into the caverns of more blinding buildings. The locals were heavy on this small street. They carried packages, food, and children through a busy open marketplace. With the pedestrians, booths, and parked cars, Dorothy realized they couldn't fit the car through at this speed. The car still went forward. Will was not stopping.

Like a child jumping through a massive pile of leaves, he destroyed a vendor's booth. Fresh meats and pieces of wood smacked against the car as they exploded through. The vendor dove for his life into a nearby shop.

They continued, this time nearly hitting a family as they ran for cover. The fender broke through the front of another booth, knocking over its awning, and then bounced off a parked wagon full of produce.

The gauntlet of Washington Heights passed through another major street immediately ahead. Squinting, Dorothy noted it was 145th Street. After plowing through another crowd of pedestrians, Will accelerated out onto the next street, veering left. With no idea of what she'd see, she clenched her hands into fists, slightly conscious of Will also bracing himself.

The car was launched several feet into the air at the mouth of the intersection due to an unexpected bump where the streets met. She let out a frightened scream when the car landed with a wrenching grinding sound from the undercarriage. Will squealed the car back under control and accelerated.

The other sedan was now coming head-on, and she understood that their pursuers must have taken a faster route to get here. Another wave of panic washed over her body as she realized Will was accelerating. The sedan veered into him as he passed and knocked the rear fender. Dorothy could see Adams' eyes at the wheel as they passed.

The impact was enough to spin the car out of control. New York rotated around them and Dorothy's vision fell in and out of focus. Will sent the wheel into a hard left, managing to stop the spin. Disoriented and slightly queasy, she looked up at her surroundings. Intersection ahead. Apartments. Stunned bystanders. Cautiously passing blue coupé. Where was the … ? The car had stalled.

They lunged forward from a sudden impact from behind.

Silence.

"Does the car work?" Dorothy asked in a whisper.

Will shrugged.

He started it and slammed on the accelerator. It did still work and almost too well. They spun into the crowded intersection of 145th and Lenox. Half a dozen cars screeched to spinning halts while another half dozen ran into each other. Will escaped the carnage, but only barely, and turned right on Harlem. It was a concrete road, which set their bodies at ease for a moment.

She checked the mirror and saw that the other sedan was stuck behind the mess Will had left at the intersection. Not as confident as she looked, she turned back to the front. More buildings walled off her vision of the side streets, but she could see a clear path ahead until the river.

"Where are we going?" she asked.

"Palace Hotel."

"Palace Hotel? What's there?"

"A friend."

They hadn't lost them. The sedan drove like a black arrow out of a forest of buildings next to them. They'd somehow found a better route. Without another word, Will drove, the sedan coming in close behind them. Unable to control the compulsion, Dorothy checked the mirror. A man was leaning out of the passenger's side window of the other sedan with a gun.

There was a loud blast immediately followed by the sound of a ricocheting bullet.

"They're just trying to stop us. Not kill us," Will stated.

"Why are you so certain?"

"We know where the treasure is."

She didn't know if he was joking or serious. Either way, his answer enraged her more. He took a left at a bridge, presumably to get away from the sedan.


Will threw the car into the traffic on a busy stretch and raced forward, trying to place their location. Madison Bridge was in the rearview mirror. The river was to the left.

The tiny urban streets were nearly impossible to drive through. The closer to Manhattan they got, the narrower the corridors became. He had very little control of the car but sped through the district anyway. He was very close to Central Park and so took a ninety-degree turn at 106th. Will completely lost control at the intersection, and the car spun wildly, colliding with a storefront.

The sedan was nowhere to be seen.

He took her hand, and they jumped out of the car into the storefront. It looked like a butcher's stand.

The proprietor was shouting insults as a newsboy ducked out of the way. The tirade stopped when he saw Will march out of the car with his torn clothes and bleeding head wound. He backed off and ran back into his store, presumably to call the police.

Dorothy and Will turned the corner. The sedan was bouncing through an alley toward them. One of the men in the backseat put his arm out of the car and fired a gun. At first, Will didn't know what it was because it had a silencer, but when the bullet ricocheted off a brick wall next to them, he knew exactly what it was.

He yanked Dorothy back toward the store they'd crashed into. Looking around, he relaxed a little when he saw the many places they could hide. He chose one. They dove into a basement boutique adjacent to the butcher. Crouching in the staircase, they didn't notice a woman approach them from behind.

She asked them something in Spanish.

Will stood up confidently and helped Dorothy to her feet.

"Sorry, ma'am, my wife fell on her way down," he said.

"Ah, señor, I hope she is fine." The woman was skeptical, eyeing their ruined clothes.

They were in a clothing boutique with upscale designs. They were not too far from the wealthy part of town now, although still a bit too north. The immigrants ruled this part of New York, but Manhattanites still loved to come up here and indulge in what they considered to be quaint boutiques. Will escorted Dorothy to some racks in the back and then blankly browsed, conscious of the fact the sedan was parked directly above them.

"What do we do?" she whispered.

"Wait it out. They want our deaths to look like an accident."

"Will. They were shooting at us."

"Intimidation."

"It worked. I'm intimidated."

Will looked around and saw two dark-suited men enter the boutique. They immediately and inconspicuously pocketed their firearms and looked around as if browsing. The Cuban woman greeted them, but they didn't respond. One absentmindedly picked up a dress while staring at them.

"Don't move," he whispered.

Dorothy stared at the rack of clothes in front of her, breathless. Will squeezed her hand tightly and went through possible scenarios in his mind.

The men were methodically closing in on them, checking price tags and browsing as they went. What would they do when they got to the back of the store? He wasn't sure they even had a plan. They were probably just keeping them in eyesight, waiting for a window to act.

He noticed when one man turned his pursuit toward the proprietor, who was reading a magazine at the register. He was going to remove their obstacle. There wasn't much time to react.

Will quickly scanned the back wall and noticed a back door. It would lead into an alley behind the boutique, where the rest of the men would surely be waiting. They'd have to leave through the front. Putting together his memories of what was immediately outside, he remembered an apartment building, a café, and the butcher they'd crashed into.

If they went to the apartment, they could be trapped. They'd have to go across the street and escape through the adjacent alley. None of their options seemed very realistic. Will saw the man nearly arrive at the register. He had a handkerchief in his hand.

There was no time.

Grabbing Dorothy's hand tightly, he ran out the back door. As he suspected, the sedan was parked in the alley with the three other men waiting inside. They immediately started the engine. He could see Adams behind the wheel.

"Run!"

The litter-covered alley was difficult to run through. Gunfire sounded around them—really close. A tuft of asphalt exploded directly in front of them. They were aiming now.

Will and Dorothy sprinted through the alley, almost making it to Park Avenue, where light traffic grumbled along. They would be safe if they could only make it there. He heard the car coming from behind and more gunshots.

Will responded by throwing Dorothy down and jumping on top of her. He could sense the vehicle coming directly behind them. Another gunshot. Debris exploded next to his head, sending brick sparks onto his face.

The sedan was coming to a stop. Dorothy was now on her feet, and this time she was dragging him. Will stumbled to his feet and they ran, the three men in close pursuit. Adams was now taking aim.

They ducked into another alley and ran to the end of it, taking another right. Will was becoming winded. More gunshots. They continued to run. As they left the mouth of the alley, they saw Central Park. The tourist crowds would save them. They ran into the crowds around the park, trying to become yet another set of New Yorkers.

Keeping his head down, Will checked behind. The other two now accompanied the three men from the alley. They scanned the crowd, hesitating. It was working. The men couldn't find them.

Their plan would only be good for a few minutes, so Will thought quickly. Dorothy pointed to passing cabs. Of course. New York. They ran and jumped into the backseat of one as it pulled up.

"The Palace Hotel," Will said in between breaths.

The cab driver, slightly annoyed at their abrupt entrance, raised an even more annoyed eyebrow at their appearance. He muttered insults under his breath and drove straight ahead.

Will took Dorothy by the cheeks and looked into her frightened eyes.

"Are you okay?"

"I think so. You?"

"For now."

# FORTY

Exhausted, filthy, and bleeding, the two managed to walk into the Palace Hotel without being thrown out. This was certainly one of Dorothy's biggest concerns. Her hard exterior began to crack a little. She couldn't take much more of this. Ever since Montreal, her life had been in a state of constant peril.

She'd break the news that she still had the key sooner or later. Perhaps later. Although he'd done a great deal to keep her alive, she didn't want to see Will angry. Military men had very bad tempers, she supposed. In hindsight, she wasn't sure why she'd kept it from him. Perhaps she didn't fully trust Will, or, more to the point, she wanted something to hold over his head in a time of crisis. Now that they were here, it seemed rather trivial.

She had to trust him now. There was no doubt in her mind that he could have left her on the train and sought out the treasure on his own. Will mentioned that his mission was her safety, and now she was convinced that was true. However, the lure of a higher duty must have distracted the knight from his mission, taking them to Oak Island. Or did it? Will said that getting the treasure was integral to her safety and ... she tried not to think about her sister and father. God help her if they were in trouble.

Skirting the strange glances of the bellmen and front desk clerks, they jogged up four flights of stairs. She wanted to ask why they didn't simply take the lift, but she knew better. After all of this, Will likely wouldn't want to be trapped. They stopped at the end of one of the hotel's decadent hallways. Two men in very nice suits and fedoras stood outside the door. They gave curious looks to each other as the couple approached, then one recognized Will.

# FORTY-ONE

"What in the name of God happened to you?" Rocky asked from under his fedora and behind a stony face. Muscles kept his suit from fitting properly, and his thick neck bulged out on all sides of a tight shirt collar. A crew cut was hidden beneath the fedora, but Will could see evidence of it from the peach fuzz sneaking out down the back of his head.

"Good to see you, Rocky."

They shook hands.

"Wait here."

The goon stepped into the room and closed the door behind him. It had been a year since Will had met Charles "Lucky" Luciano in Havana, and he hoped that not too much had changed during that time. Knowing full well that the crime boss should be in Italy as part of a deal he made with the U.S. government, he also knew he had New York operations that needed tending to. Lucky had operations in Havana as well, and after the Havana Conference, he needed to center his business there. This old ally would be their quickest route to Bermuda.

Rocky opened the door and said, "If you vouch for your lady friend, Lucky will see you."

"Don't worry, Rocky, she's with me."

The thick-necked man nodded and stepped aside so they could

enter. Dorothy would undoubtedly be nervous, so he took her hand. It was cool and dry; perhaps he'd underestimated her ... or maybe she didn't make the connection about who they were seeing. Only high-ranking members of the Commission knew of Lucky's New York office, and the only reason the Poor Fellow-Soldiers knew about it was because the two groups had had to work together a great deal during the war. It was the Order that convinced the Truman administration and consequently Governor Thomas Dewey to release Lucky to Italy. His connections and the Syndicate in general kept a huge number of foreign threats out of the States. Once again, the Poor Fellow-Soldiers had been called to arms against both National Socialists and the Communists during the first part of the decade, and their work had sealed a permanent relationship with both Washington and the Organization.

This, of course, was all top-secret. Not even the Vatican knew that the Poor Fellow-Soldiers worked with Luciano and the Organization, even though it happened under their nose. Will knew quite well. He'd worked alongside Lucky in several New York operations. They were brothers-in-arms and had an immense amount of respect for each other. Things were more difficult since the Havana Conference. The U.S. turned on Luciano once they realized he was violating the terms of his parole. Hawks in the administration had also lost patience with the old ways, wanting to reform the government and its policy against the Organization.

Will didn't like their methods, but as with any country or powerful society, one had to create diplomatic relationships to survive, and the Italian mafia was staying. He was in no position to judge their methods anyway. The Order also worked above and outside all governments for their own agenda, and although they were far less brutal than the mafia, bloodshed and secret warfare were just as common. After their recent conflict with the Jesuits, there could be no discernible difference between their operations and the Organization's.

It was no surprise that in his darkest hour, he had to seek out Lucky Luciano for help.

As with any world leader, it was very nerve-racking to meet person to person. A quiet and profound air of power circulated among these men, and Luciano was no different. It was ironic to realize that he felt the same amount of nerves when meeting with Lucky as he did with Harry Truman. Of course, that meeting took place under far different circumstances: Will and his team were being commended for their work in Europe.

Luciano's room at the Palace Hotel was humbling. Three chandeliers lit up the opulent suite, and a wall of windows displayed Manhattan's forest of skyscrapers. A full bar covered one end, and cocktail tables circulated throughout, presenting a club-like atmosphere. Two other rooms were closed off, but based on the furnishings of the main room, the bedrooms must have been unbelievable. Lucky Luciano stood in the center of the room smoking a cigar. His hair was unwashed, and he wore a silk bathrobe with an Oriental design. It dawned on Will that it was still morning.

Luciano held a newspaper and what looked like a brandy in his thick hands. Dark eyebrows in a firm frown framed a proud, expressionless face. Faded scars still showed on his chin, and caverns of experience radiated from his eyes. Glancing upward at them for only a second, he returned to his paper.

"Who's your friend?" he asked.

"Dorothy Wilkinson. She is under my protection."

Lucky looked up at her, examining her face and eyes.

"I should tell you, sense you say that she is under your protection, that perhaps this may not be the safest place for her. I'm probably being watched."

"If anyone knew you were here, you'd have been shipped back to Sicily by now," Will stated.

"True." His thoughts were interrupted as he looked them over again. "You both look terrible. I have clothes in the wardrobe and a washroom you can use. It's difficult to do business when you don't look your best."

Always the gentleman, Luciano opened one of the closed doors, giving an obliging smile to Dorothy. Taking the hint, she went inside, and Lucky closed the door behind her.

"She looks scared," he said.

"If I told you what we've been through in the past few days, you wouldn't believe it."

"You're welcome to my clothes. They may be big for you, but it's better than this."

"Thank you, Mr. Luciano."

Lucky took a puff from his cigar and finished whatever article he was reading before setting the paper down. Pulling two shot glasses from the bar, he uncapped a bottle of whiskey and poured them both a glass. This was a ritual Will had participated in before; business was always discussed over drinks. Social inhibitions left, and strong men were sorted from the weak ones. Deals were made or broken over the acceptance or refusal of a drink.

"What brings you here, Sir Shakespeare?"

"The knights were attacked and divided. The grand master is dead. So are most of the commanders. I was left with only a single mission: to return Miss Wilkinson to Bermuda."

They took drinks, symbolizing that the conversation could continue. Will had just disclosed the basics, and Luciano signaled he was prepared to accept them and hear more instead of refusing help.

Will continued after Lucky filled the glasses again.

"There's a hurricane on the way to the Caribbean. We believe it will destroy a very important artifact that we protect. I need help getting to Havana so we can retrieve it in time."

Lucky didn't drink, taking a moment to think.

"Who did it?"

"I believe it was the society."

He still didn't drink. This made Will nervous. It was extremely possible that Lucky's Catholic allegiance could get in the way here. Generally, Luciano and the Syndicate worked in close concert with the Jesuits and other Vatican groups.

The pause seemed to last hours before Luciano finally took a drink. Will followed, and Lucky poured another.

"It's not them. Not entirely," Lucky said. "The society does not want your artifacts. You should be dead already."

That was a good point Will hadn't thought about. Perhaps it was the nature of the past few hours, but the entire pursuit made absolutely no sense. If the Jesuits was truly involved, they would have been dead, and the hurricane would have been allowed to do its damage. The nemesis would at last be gone, and their secrets with it. Someone else was operating here, and Will very much doubted it was Adams alone.

"This I will do," Lucky said, "but I must keep my word with God. I help you because you're up against an enemy I do not respect. Your other enemy, though, has no secrets with me; therefore, I have none with them."

The ball was now in Will's court. Luciano would send them to Havana, but he'd also tell the society. It was a good compromise for a man in his position, and one that could prove deadly to both Will and Dorothy. He was now the one considering. They had no other way out. Any traditional means would be spotted directly by the authorities. All of Will's networks were crushed or overseas. Luciano was his last card.

Will took the drink, and without another word on the subject, the deal was made.

# FORTY-TWO

The Palace Hotel had all the amenities of an actual palace, and Luciano's room was the *crème de la crème* of the hotel. Three full baths with two bedrooms and a master bedroom; each tub could easily fit a small family, and the selection of soaps and sundries was staggering. Dorothy took advantage of the wet bar placed strategically by the bath. She had no idea what time it was and didn't care. The boys were likely drinking out there without her anyway.

She drew a very hot bath using a combination of scents and soaps until suds rose high into the air. Peeling off her days-old clothes was like skinning herself. The stench of caverns, cargo trains, and New York streets puffed into a medley of more prominent aromas. She sunk heavily into the bath with her brandy, watching the suds pop around her. The water melted her, and in the next moment she found her eyes closed and the last few days floating away from her.

For the first time since she'd left Bermuda she felt safe, which was ironic considering she was only steps away from the world's most notorious gangster. She knew quite well who Lucky Luciano was, but it didn't bother her. After all, meeting the mafia seemed somewhat normal. It also didn't surprise her that Shakespeare had relationships with the likes of Luciano. A secret society would have to mingle with other secret societies somehow. It was just fortunate for them they were on the mafia's good side—or at least a negotiable one.

She tried to let the last few days waft away in the prickling water around her. It rushed through her memory, and at last her thoughts landed on her father and sister. They'd be going to them very soon. Their safety was no doubt in question, but she knew also that without the key they couldn't get far. The only trouble was they'd try to get at her family, so she'd turn over the key.

She wondered why they hadn't found the key on her or thought to look for it. It was as if they'd been quickly shoved inside with no time to spare. She also wondered why they wanted to know if this Sam Adams was going rogue, and if the other bad guys were wise to it. Were they being pursued by more than one party?

Glancing down at the pile of moldy, torn, and bloody clothes on the bathroom floor, she realized she was also withholding something from Will. She hadn't told him about the key perhaps because of lack of trust. She trusted him now. She had to. He was all she had until her family was safe.

She peeked over the tub and dragged her clothes near. Reaching into the front pocket, she pulled the key out. It was a simple skeleton key—nothing dramatic at all. It was somewhat large, but small enough to keep hidden. The moment she'd retrieved the box from the cavern, she'd pocketed the key. It was her safety net and bartering tool. That seemed like ages ago. They were in a far different world now. The hurricane would be coming soon, and the enemy would be rounding up her loved ones. It would be war.

Those thoughts finally found their way into the bath, and with another sip of brandy, she felt like nothing was wrong. Then there was a pounding on the bathroom door.

# FORTY-THREE

Adams lit a cigarette as Thomas pounded on the door. He cast a sideward glance at Luciano, who still hadn't dressed, glaring from the other side of the room. Four others of the society looked around the room, and he'd just dispatched another into the other closed room. His glance turned into a stare as he realized Luciano was giving him a cold look.

"Leave the lady alone," he said.

"I know the Poor Knights came to you, Luciano. If you want your alliances secure, you should tell me where they went."

"My alliances aren't with you," he said plainly. "Perhaps the Roman Curia would like to know your activities? In fact, I was going to meet a cardinal in Havana next week. Maybe I'll call him now."

Somehow the Sicilian knew Adams wasn't working for the Barrister. This made Adams very nervous, but he had to stay collected. This was his moment of control, and he wouldn't let some criminal intimidate him. It didn't matter anyway. The Barrister already knew about his betrayal and was after him. But when he had the Grail in his hands, he'd have the power of a hundred nations behind him. World leaders would do whatever he said ... with the help of his master, of course.

*If only Willy knew who was really behind this operation.*

Adams now needed to make sure the loose ends were tied up. Having Shakespeare and Wilkinson still at large was a huge liability. His contacts in Bermuda had already apprehended Walter Wilkinson, so they were no longer needed. He had the key and the map, and he'd soon have the treasure. He'd keep Wilkinson obliged to him with the head of his daughter, even though that head would be removed before the day was up.

This gangster would bend. They all did.

"Thomas, break down the door," Adams said, still watching Luciano.

"Where are your manners?"

A woman was inside, and she screeched at the entry. She was wearing only a towel, and Adams looked her over with quiet amusement. Truthfully, he'd never had a good look at Dorothy Wilkinson, so there was no way he could identify her in this state. It was immaterial. Chances were this one was her, and if it wasn't, he'd keep looking until he found her.

"Kill her," he said.

Luciano had a pistol pointing at Adams faster than he could turn his head.

"You sure you want to do that?"

"You're in good standing with the society, Luciano. Don't fuck it up."

There was no hesitation. Lucky Luciano pulled the trigger. Adams' heart jumped. Numbness fell from his forehead. The world flickered around him. He collapsed, and it was all gone.

# FORTY-FOUR

Will jumped out from the pantry at the sound of the gunshot. Dressed in a nicely tailored suit and freshly showered, he was ready for action. Adams was dead on the tile floor, and his goons were staring at him, not speaking or moving.

Luciano was already putting his gun on the table and taking a puff of his cigar.

"Don't speak that way in front of a lady," he said to the corpse before turning to Will. "We are all friends here, Sir Shakespeare."

Blinking in confusion, Will stood, unmoving.

Luciano continued, "Gentlemen, go to the Barrister and tell him what Mr. Adams was up to. Tell him that you were lied to and were acting under what you believed to be his orders. Tell him to call me, and I will tell him the same. Tell him I owed Sir Shakespeare a favor, and he wanted passage to Havana. Tell him I'll do one better and send him to Bermuda."

Dorothy, still clad in a hastily wrapped towel, gasped loudly.

"I'm sorry, Miss Wilkinson," Luciano said. "This is how it must be."

Without a word, the members of the society left the room.

Will, surprised his nemesis had been so easily put down, stood for a moment before offering Luciano a handshake.

"I owe you."

"It's nothing."

Dorothy couldn't handle it. She jumped into the room.

"This son of a bitch has turned us in!"

"Miss Wilkinson," Will tried. "He has alliances to preserve. Believe me, this is a favor."

"A favor?"

"I can see you are very upset," Luciano said. "You will find some decent apparel in the wardrobe. I trust you don't want to be seen like this."

Stopping dead in her tracks, she gave Will a curious look and then disappeared back into the bathroom.

"I'll explain," Will said.

"Know this," Luciano said quietly. "This man was not acting alone. Your true enemy is still at large. I know you fear the actions of the Society of Jesus, but in the end, they are the only ones you can trust."

Will put a fedora on his head for the first time in days. "I hope this hasn't been too much trouble."

"You don't have much time," Luciano answered and handed him his pistol.

Bermuda, United Kingdom
September 13, 1947.

# FORTY-FIVE

Dorothy wanted to put New York behind her. The whole affair had been a whirlwind of violence and terror culminating in desperation. She stood there and watched her sole source of protection hand their position over to the enemy. Will tried to explain that negotiating with the likes of the mafia was delicate, and because Luciano had good relations with both the Poor Fellow-Soldiers and the Society of Jesus, he had to compromise them while saving face. It was political, and it made her angry. There was no reason in the world Luciano could have turned a blind eye after hearing about the actions of his "so-called" allies.

She couldn't pretend to know the intricacies of the way these people worked, but she did know that her family's lives were on the line because of these politics. Will suddenly didn't seem so trustworthy. She kept distance between them and decided to keep the key secret. Perhaps she'd need to barter down the road. Who knew what his true motives were at this point?

The sting of the affair wore off as they boarded the passenger ship to Bermuda. Leaving, the world-famous New York skyline embedded itself into her memory. The sun was rising in the east and cast an amazing orange aura over the buildings, bringing them into an ominous stature, silhouetted against a perfect blue sky. The Statue of Liberty reflected the sun with an awesome brilliance, properly fulfilling her iconic obligation in Dorothy's mind.

They had first-class quarters just below the captain's cabin. The whole trip was apparently paid for, and the sheer luxurious nature of their accommodations caused her anger to quickly slip away. She'd only seen luxury such as this from afar as flocks of European and American tourist raided Bermuda every month. It had seemed decadent to her, but experiencing it firsthand was quite different. Everyone addressed her formally and didn't allow her to inconvenience herself in any way at all.

Will remained quiet, seemingly accepting her cold distance and perhaps sensing she wasn't at all satisfied with their situation. Even after she warmed up, however, he kept his distance. The luxe accommodations were only a distraction from the difficult times ahead. She didn't know what to expect when she returned home, but she knew some very powerful people were after them and whatever secrets her father held on their property.

They each had their own bedroom and shared a sitting room, where Will set up camp on a large sofa. He unpacked a few things Luciano had given to them before they left. One case held a Thompson machine gun, and the sight of it startled her. She was immediately brought back to the carnage in Montreal. Shuddering at what their future might hold, she disappeared into her room as he continued to unpack.

Resting on the bed, she caught a glimpse of the Atlantic as it passed by. Fortunately, the weather was nice, but she knew full well in four days' time the hurricane would be right on top of them. Although she had no access to news reports, the initial findings suggested it wouldn't be a little one. In fact, some thought the hurricane could turn into the biggest one in a hundred years. If her family was safe, they would have already made proper preparations. They'd put valuables in the shelter, and her father would have stocked up on supplies. If something had gone wrong though, there was no telling how much preparation had been left unfinished. Clearly, the people involved here were quite unaware of the horrific effects hurricanes could have.

As the sun came into full view over the ship, Dorothy drifted into much-needed sleep.

# FORTY-SIX

All his guns, ammo, and equipment were neatly packed into a shoulder bag. He would need them. They were walking directly into a war zone. Luciano's generosity was short-lived, and Will knew full well that after they docked in King's Wharf, the enemy would be waiting for them. His only consolation was that he would at last see who the ringleader for this morbid operation was. He wanted to see the bastard who thought that an ancient organization's death and the preservation of mystical human history were less important than their own wealth and power.

Watching Adams die had hardened him. He knew now that he was up against the real foe and that an equally strong enemy was also on his heels. Whoever was betraying the Order would be matched only by the calculating efficiency of this man Luciano and Adams called "the Barrister." Even if they could get the treasure out of the hands of whatever madman was trying to get it, Will would have to keep them and the treasure safe from the Barrister.

There were two very major concerns that had an annoying habit of popping into whatever thought he conjured. One, the key was not on Adams's person. The box was. This meant either the bastard had hidden it somewhere, or it hadn't been in the box to begin with. In both cases, getting to the treasure would be very, very difficult. That was assuming he could find the treasure, of course, but that was the other concern. He had no idea where the map was or how he'd locate it. Secretly hoping that the Wilkinsons had something to do with it, he'd managed to keep the concern at bay. Now that they were en route to Bermuda, it was all he could think about. He was going to save a treasure without knowing its location and without having a key to unlock it.

Useless as it seemed, he knew it was inevitable. Although his prime objective was to keep Dorothy Wilkinson alive, he also knew it was directly related to what was on her property. No matter the outcome, if she died, he'd have to be dead already. The remaining Poor Fellow-Soldiers, knights or squires, wouldn't find out about the travesty for months perhaps, and by then, whoever was operating this would already have had them killed.

A nagging worry crept up apart from those concerns. Will couldn't figure out why Adams would keep them alive only to try to kill them later. Something in their plans must have changed. His suspicion was that they would find out soon enough. Their enemy would be waiting for them, and Will wouldn't be surprised if the Wilkinsons were already dead.

Dorothy's coldness was natural, and he thought perhaps he shouldn't try to change her mood. In due time, she'd learn to trust him and his methods. Unless one lived in this secret world, one couldn't understand that what Luciano did was a favor ... or at least the best possible thing he could have done.

All they could do now was wait. The closer Bermuda came, the less Will could sleep, until after three days he hadn't slept at all. On the last day of their trip, he wasn't surprised to see Dorothy up at three in the morning as well.

# FORTY-SEVEN

It should have been a blissful three days. They'd been afforded every luxury the passenger ship had to offer—drinks, meals, clothing, cigarettes, music, and even dancing. Will gave Dorothy an obligatory dance on the last night of their cruise, but neither was very interested in it. Despite all the star treatment they'd received, Bermuda was on the horizon, and the enemy waited for them there.

Now they both waited over fresh coffee in their sitting room, watching the stars. Ocean air that early in the morning had a bite to it, even this far south, and Will retrieved a blanket for Dorothy as they relaxed on the sofa. Sipping their coffee quietly, Will offered the most comforting expression he could. She returned his look with concerned eyes, and Will could almost perceive tears in them.

"It will be okay," he stated.

"You don't sound so sure."

He wasn't. But he knew that he'd stop at nothing to remove this problem from her life. It wasn't just his mission but also the culmination of everything he stood for and was trained for. There couldn't be a better person to get her out of this—except for Franklin. It wasn't the first time Will had wished he was there; he could use some guidance from his mentor.

But Franklin wasn't there. He'd been killed in Montreal along with the other leaders of his knighthood. Will was on his own ... left to his own devices. Knowing trust was a luxury; he wasn't even certain he could trust himself. There were too many burning questions. And the one he was protecting ... what was she hiding?

Her eyes were distant, involved in a whole line of thoughts perhaps similar to his own. She hadn't spoken much on their journey, and there were many questions. Why did the Order trust her family to safeguard the most important relics in human history? Why had he been specifically instructed to keep her safe? Did they have the map? How were they going to get in without the key? Who was behind this whole mess? How long would it take for the Barrister to get there? Were the other Wilkinsons still alive?

They sat quietly throughout the morning. Breakfast was served at nine, and they ate it together, all the while watching the oncoming island grow ever closer on the horizon. After the sun rose, it was remarkably warm and clear. Will had to remind himself that they were hours away from a hurricane.

"Listen," he said at last. "We need to be upfront with each other. There can be nothing between us. I need very much to trust you, and I'm sure you need the same from me."

Leaning in close, ignoring the clatter of dishes and glasses, he continued, "I am very skilled, but I may not be enough. The Society of Jesus is out to completely eliminate the treasure and us. There is a rogue group that is after the treasure, and we're in the way. After we leave this ship, we'll be in a great deal of danger. I have to tell you that I don't know how your family is or even if I can save them."

She looked as if a dagger had been shoved into her heart.

"We will go to them, but know that my mission is to save you. Not to get the treasure, not to protect your household, and not to keep your family safe. Of course, I will try to do these things, but if any of those actions in any way put you in direct danger, I am obligated to abort."

There was a pained silence. He wanted to say more, but perhaps he'd said enough.

"Thank you for being candid, Sir Shakespeare," she said at last. "And allow me to say this, you may be tied to me through some arbitrary mission, but I am not tied to you. I intend to do everything within my power to make sure my family is safe with or without you. Because of your mission, I suspect I will be doing it with your help."

She leaned in close as well. He could see the strength in her eyes.

Gentle wafts of lavender whispered around him.

"And may I remind you, Sir Shakespeare, that it is your lawless organization that put my family in this situation to begin with."

He retorted only with "We have laws. They are just a bit older than the ones you're accustomed to."

"Are you suggesting that I'm not cut out for this? Sir Shakespeare, I know that this treasure of yours is important to humanity ... or at least you believe it is. There are those in the world who treasure things other than knowledge."

"This may be true, but you must understand the weight of what we protect. Thousands of years of wars were fought for this knowledge; it is not to be trivialized."

"Wars were fought for many things, and only a handful of those things made those wars worth it. Don't value your precious commodities so highly, sir. You may lose sight of what's actually important."

The point slammed him back into his seat. Openly confused, his stare was a cross between admiration and indignation. How can she completely disregard the whole point of the knighthood?

"Spiritual gnosis, Miss Wilkinson. I value the progress of man's divine future more than anything else."

"Why value it? If man's future is written with the same materials as man's past, what is there to preserve? You have this global ideal ... this notion that human spirituality will in some way save us all. Human spirituality has done a fine job in destroying us all. You may find solace in that thinking, Sir Shakespeare, but me ... I must find human miracles on a much smaller scale. The kindness a father has shown his daughter, for example."

It hit home. Her steady gaze said it all. This wasn't about anything but her loved ones. He blinked into submission. It was difficult to understand how finding the treasure could not be a priority, but then again she wasn't a Poor Fellow-Soldier. She was a civilian. Perhaps these things were kept secret not to preserve the secret itself but because others wouldn't understand the secret. Or worse, wouldn't care about it.

Yet there were men who wanted to kill her for it.

"I give you my word, Miss Wilkinson, I will do everything I can to make sure your family is safe. But my obligation to your safety supersedes that. I hope we understand each other."

"Sir Shakespeare, I don't give a damn what you do. This isn't about you. It never was."

With those words, she left the table. After working in spy networks in Nazi Germany, fighting secret battles in Cuba, working to eliminate nationalist control in Vietnam, combating the Axis fronts of the war, it was those words that tore down his military shell. He sat, broken, absentmindedly poking at his meal. Had this woman called into question everything he believed in?

He felt better after more coffee. Spending a good amount of time regaining his composure, he left a tip and retired to the room, hoping to find Dorothy there.

# FORTY-EIGHT

Rage got the better of her. She was sick of being treated like a child—or worse, like an ignorant woman who was tagging along because she didn't know better. There was no doubt that the Western world treated people this way, but in Bermuda things were different. This was her turf and her home. This was her family they were talking about. The ridiculous notion that this soldier for an obscure secret society would in any way impede her from helping her family was infuriating to her.

She went back to the room, knowing that he'd follow. It didn't matter; she'd gotten it off her chest, and now, as he had wanted, there was nothing between them. She didn't want anything to do with this treasure anyway. Her objective was far simpler. She wanted things back the way they were.

When Will returned, she didn't look at him and instead poured a glass of whatever red wine had been left for the passengers. He wouldn't have any. With a somewhat aggressive motion, he took her shoulders.

Dorothy, already upset, didn't like that one bit. She threw daggers at him with her eyes and clutched her wine glass as if it were a weapon.

"Miss Wilkinson, listen to me."

She did. He would get one sentence.

"You are dealing with organizations older than most nations."

That wasn't good enough. She wrenched free and backed away so she could take a slug of the wine. It numbed her senses.

"Sir Shakespeare, I don't believe you can handle this any more than I can. So if it's all the same to you, I believe we should part ways after we land."

"I can't do that."

"You very well can, Sir. Shakespeare, and I demand that you do so. My time with you has been spent under fire and breaking values I hold very dear. You preach a great deal about my safety, but you dragged me into the worst possible situations and with the worst outcomes. Not for my safety, sir, but for your precious history and this so-called treasure that is on the minds of dangerous and reckless secret societies who believe they are above the law."

There, she said it.

Her comments obviously took him off guard. He sat, lit a cigarette, and reflected for a moment, his eyes not leaving hers.

"I promised your family's safety ..."

"Only as a pacifier, and it's a promise I doubt you can keep."

"You have every right to be upset. But don't let your anger cloud your judgment. If you refuse my help, you're walking into certain death."

"It isn't me they're after."

"Why are you so sure?"

"The only threat I saw with my own eyes was murdered right in front of me by a gangster. Any threats you speak of have to do with you, not me."

He shook his head, frustration taking over. "You have to trust me."

"Trust you? To what end? So I can end up in another high-speed car chase? Or drowned in some Godforsaken pirate cave? You must take me for a fool, Sir Shakespeare."

He fell silent, but his eyes were earnest—almost emphatic. It was as if she'd slapped him. It was one of the strongest emotions she'd ever seen on his cold face. A spike of guilt suddenly drilled into her anger. He'd been a bodyguard to her, taking her from the bloodbath in Montreal and leading her directly to the people who could help the most. She simply couldn't ignore all the danger he'd put her in, though.

Except that he believed if the treasure was still there, her family was in danger. What if he were right? She'd seen enough to believe almost anything now. A certain part of her wanted to trust him. Could she so easily concede?

"We will need a compromise," she said at last. "You take me to my family, and from then on, your mission is accomplished. You have no obligation to me after that."

"I'm sorry, Miss Wilkinson," he said, his neutral expression returning. "And with all due respect, you are not the one who determines my assignments." He paused uncomfortably and then added, "I'll let you pack in private."

Finishing his cigarette, he walked out the door, leaving Dorothy to wonder what was in store for them and how he could possibly do what he claimed. A more prominent thought rose in her mind, however, and Dorothy began to seriously wonder why she was so important to this knighthood. She was a colonial daughter, raised in paradise. It was clear there was something about all this that she didn't know, and she was beginning to suspect Shakespeare didn't know either. What other secrets did this knighthood carry?

As Bermuda snaked into her view over the deck, she knew that those secrets would be revealed soon enough, and it was likely she wouldn't like the truth any more than she did the mystery.

# FORTY-NINE

The captain informed the passengers he had just learned that a hurricane would pass by Bermuda by nightfall. This news threw Will into an alarmed state. He had no idea they were that close to their destination. Doing the math in his head, he realized he'd been aware of this eventuality, but during their struggles to get here, it had somehow slipped his mind how imminent the danger was. The captain, in an effort to avoid the worst of the storm, was sailing to Fort Lauderdale to seek shelter for a few days before the storm hit Florida. The landing at Bermuda, then, would be temporary, only long enough to refill supplies before heading off. It would be time enough for them to get onto the island, however, and that was Will's sole concern.

When they came into King's Wharf, yet another realization brought Will nearly to his breaking point. Peering out his cabin, he could see a ten-man-strong police force waiting on the dock. There was only one reason for them to be waiting for this particular ship. While he knew they'd eventually be intercepted, he'd underestimated his enemy's ability to mobilize. Briefly wondering if the Barrister or the phantom enemy had dispatched these police to retrieve the Poor Fellow-Soldiers' treasure, he decided it didn't matter much. They could not be caught; it wasn't a jail cell waiting for them. A brief scan over the heads of the policemen suggested that whoever was commanding them was either not present or not in sight.

Probably not in sight.

It was very possible the Barrister was already there. He'd been given plenty of notice, and with his resources he would have access to a direct flight to Bermuda. The colonial police waiting for them would surely have to have been dispatched by someone within the United Kingdom's network, and there was no doubt the Barrister had such connections. He couldn't begin to wonder whether these cops belonged to his phantom enemy, not knowing the nature of the foe. At this point it didn't matter who sent them. He would find out soon enough.

Dorothy came up from behind to see what he was looking at. Watching her bite her lower lip, Will realized she wasn't showing fear but thoughtfulness. Before he could speak, she said, "We'll have to leave with the crew. That's our only chance." She paused and offered a raised eyebrow. "Unless you want to go out with guns blazing."

"Only when absolutely necessary."

They had very little time to mobilize, but her plan sparked an idea.

"The kitchen."

They both took their belongings, amounting to two bags each, and made their way as calmly as possible down to the main deck. The crew were still offering cocktails and tea as they came in to dock, and that made their next step much easier. Slipping unnoticed into the kitchen, they were at once surrounded by hectic hustle  and bustle. Cooks shouted out orders as they threw platters onto the serving counter, while servers slipped the orders out.

At first no one noticed them until one cook barked at them from behind the counter, "You aren't allowed back here."

Will ignored him even after he chased them into the back office.

"Hey!" the cook shouted.

Will at once turned around with a fierceness he rarely used and that was completely feigned. "My father is the owner of this vessel, and I insist that you speak more gently in front of my wife."

The cook paused and then recoiled. "Yes, Mr. Morris, I didn't recognize you. My apologies, please."

The cook went back into the kitchen, having far more important things with which to concern himself. Will knew quite well that most people immediately folded when faced with direct conflict.

They were in the back office with walls of lockers on either side.

They'd found the right place. Will opened up a couple of lockers and dug out uniforms. It was ideal for them. The uniforms fit nicely over their clothing and easily disguised their features. Complete with chef coats, hats, and checkered pants, the two were nearly unrecognizable.

Placing their baggage under a food cart covered with a tablecloth, Will finished the charade by planting rows of wrapped dish sets on the cart. They waited there for a full hour as the ship docked, smoking cigarettes and staying quiet. Things would start to happen very soon.

And indeed they did. The kitchen staff flew back into a frenzy of activity, barely noticing the two were there. In a few rounds of organized chaos, supplies and food were piled onto various carts and put into a single-file line on the way out. Will and Dorothy easily ended up in this line, toting their own supplies with dozens of others dressed and behaving just like them.

Before he knew it, they were on dry land once again with the police not forty yards away, completely oblivious to their presence. Hauling their supplies off to the terminal, it was easy to disappear into the crowd.

Will spotted a row of parked cars adjacent to the terminal and began burrowing his way through the crowd to get there, now toting his bags over his back. Dorothy closely followed, keeping her hand firmly cupped in his.

He needed an inconspicuous car and spied one toward the end of the lot. It was a black sedan that was nice, but not too nice. It was the sort of car a colonial would drive, but not a wealthy tourist. Tossing their bags in the back, Dorothy immediately jumped into the passenger seat, apparently having no problem with the inevitable theft that was about to occur.

Will peeled out of the lot, glancing into the rearview mirror. The police were nowhere in sight. It seemed for the first time things were starting to fall into place.

Dorothy quietly and curtly gave directions around the island. Gentle slopes with tropical trees adorned the well-manicured wharfs as they cruised away.

A short drive later, Will pulled into a secluded pebble-stone driveway. Taking the car up the drive revealed an opening between cedars. A three-story, beautifully built house came into view—British colonial design complete with red-brick arches and white pillars. Will pulled up to the front and stopped the car. Although he sensed Dorothy's urge to bolt inside, it was apparent she knew better. Will reached into his bag and pulled out a pistol.

"Come in behind me. Nothing reckless, we don't know what's in there."

"I want a weapon."

This forced a loss of composure. Will was, for the first time, furrowing his brow at her, and she was the one with the coldly neutral expression. Either something had changed in her, or it was simply that she was on her own ground now. There would be no argument. It was dangerous to give an untrained person a weapon, but it was more important that she could protect herself. Without comment, he handed her his gun and dug out another.

They simultaneously got out of the car and approached the house.

Will's nerves were heightened, as they always were before a conflict. He was accustomed to the feeling and was trained to utilize that energy for focus. After a prayer, he focused the energy into a finely crafted tool. It was so engrained into his overall technique now that he hardly thought about it.

Taking a calculated risk, he decided to go directly in. The door was unlocked, and he threw it open, holding his gun out in front.

# FIFTY

It was dark inside, which was hardly unusual. Her father would have vacated the house yesterday at news of the oncoming hurricane. It was her first signal that things could be all right. Gripping the cold pistol made her feel less sure. She felt as if letting go would be the same as throwing away a life preserver. Things were not normal inside, no matter how much she wanted to believe it.

First, the door was unlocked. That fact outweighed the issue of the darkness. Her father's keys were hanging on the hall hooks. The windows weren't boarded up. Two newspapers were sitting on the porch. The hallway carpet wasn't rolled up. There had been absolutely no preparation for this hurricane, and that was the sole reason she knew all was not well.

"Something's wrong," she whispered.

It would be in her best interest to warn Will not to let his guard down. A sideward glance revealed that he had no intention of doing so. Gripping the pistol with both hands, he swung around both corners. There was nothing there. The only place left to go was through the main hall, where they'd reach the study, kitchen, and master staircase. As they passed the study, her heart fell. Coldness gripped her body, and she forgot how to breathe.

# FIFTY-ONE

"Come in, Sir William," a quiet voice said from inside the study.

Will moved inside, instinctively bringing his aim to the source of the voice. What met his eyes stunned him so much he lost his breath. Sweat jumped from his forehead. Keeping the pistol steady, he reached over and turned on the light. Surely what he was seeing was a mistake.

An older man was tied to a leather chair positioned next to a wall-sized desk covered with a library of old books. He wore pajamas and a bathrobe, and his hair was tousled and unwashed. His mouth was taped shut, but Will could see emotion in his wide and frightened eyes. Standing to either side of him were two men in finely tailored suits and fedoras. Both had pistols in hand. He didn't immediately recognize them. It was the man smoking a cigar opposite them, leaning against a smaller desk, that grabbed his attention.

"If you want this civilian to live, you'll put down your weapons," the man said.

Will had no choice but to oblige. Dorothy dropped her gun and ran over to the man who must have been her father. She clutched him, tears rushing from her eyes. The greeting was short-lived as one of the men pulled her several feet away.

Will's attention fell on the man at the small desk. Benjamin Franklin. His mentor, guide, and leader. He was the traitor. He wanted to own the treasure rather than preserve it. He'd mobilized the knighthood's most ancient enemy to kill the grand master, destroy the Order, and leave him as the sole proprietor of the most valuable items in human history. It was Franklin who had turned his own student, Adams, against the Poor Fellow-Soldiers. The man Will respected most in life. The man he considered a father. The man he thought dead a week ago in a slaughter that had taken away all Will knew.

He had no words. Franklin knew it and so proceeded after a deep puff of his cigar.

"I didn't expect you to meet with Luciano," he said. "That put us in a pretty terrible bind. The Barrister now knows where to find us. That son of a bitch was only supposed to be useful in Canada. I didn't expect him to stick to the task like a fly on shit."

He paused.

"Pardon the language, Miss Wilkinson."

She only glared at him.

"Look, Sir William. I know what you're thinking. I've let greed take over. I've destroyed thousands of years of tradition and history, but to be frank, I don't really care. I've given this knighthood forty of my best years. I've seen four wars. I've gone through two grand masters. I'm here to tell you that none of it matters. Lofty idealism. That's it."

He turned his attention to Dorothy and attempted a smile. "Miss Wilkinson, you have nothing to worry about. Your father is leverage. I'll only kill him if Sir William doesn't do what he's asked."

Then he turned back to Will.

Will remembered those eyes as being confident and gentle, now all he saw was coldness. A monster had emerged. It was impossible to believe this was the Sir Franklin Will knew. Corruption had taken over. Greed. All oaths, work, and achievements were completely nullified. One of the oldest members of the knighthood had completely destroyed their whole purpose and unleashed the dogs to ensure it was done right.

"I need you," Franklin said, "to get the Holy Grail before the hurricane does."

"Get it yourself."

"I'd rather not. Very risky. Not even the map discloses all of the traps. I need you to ... well, set them off, so to speak, so I don't have to worry about them."

"That's the only reason you sent me out of Montreal? To come here and be your canary?" He was losing control and tried for a moment to regain his composure.

"No. Actually, I thought I had to do it by myself. I needed you to get the key. As for Miss Wilkinson, she was a patsy. I knew if she was kept alive, you'd find out about the hurricane. After that, she's relatively useless. After Adams took the key, he was going to send you to 'accidentally' die in New York. A tragic double suicide was planned to keep the authorities out of it. Adams didn't get the key, so I knew you'd come here, and that's when Mr. Wilkinson came into it."

He tossed Will a very old but still-bound book. He knew what it was—the Sinclair document disclosed it. Francis Bacon's diary. The only existing complete map of the Crystal Cave. It led straight to the hidden underground town: Drake's Harbor. Bacon named the town after his estranged and deceased father, Francis Drake, who'd begun the operation thirty years prior. The book had been kept safe in the Wilkinsons' library at the grand master's request. They knew that infiltration of the Poor Fellow-Soldiers' archives could reveal it, and so left it where no one would think to look, in a low-level Freemason's library.

"You are going to lead us to Drake's Harbor, Sir William," Franklin said, "or I will kill Mr. Wilkinson and find it myself. Now, as a good turcopolier, you will preserve the treasure at all costs, even civilian life. But I know you better. You seem to have a conscience. You also want to see the treasure safe. This should be an easy choice, but it is still a choice."

Franklin was right. In every regard he should let the Holy Grail sink rather than let it fall into the hands of the enemy. He couldn't do that. He also couldn't let Mr. Wilkinson die. He'd made a promise.

The weight of the monumental scenario crashed down upon him. He wanted desperately to fold and just let things unravel, but a quiet strength kept him standing. He knew he had no choice. He had to find this bastard his prize.

It came as a complete surprise when the tables suddenly turned on Franklin.

# FIFTY-TWO

Seeing her father bound and gagged was terrifying, but there was one important element to the scene that no one else in the room seemed to notice. Dorothy realized right away that her sister Rita was not present. Her father was fearful, but there was confidence in those eyes as well. They'd been working something out. It would take a great deal of perception to determine what their plan was, and she had little time to do it.

The conversation between Will and her father's captor bought her a few moments. Glancing around the study, she looked for clues. There were none to be seen. Cataloging the house, she wondered where her sister could have gone where she wouldn't be discovered by these apparently astute men. It was suddenly clear where she'd hidden. It was the perfect spot and one where she could observe all that was going on in the house. The hatch to the hurricane shelter was beneath the master staircase. Dorothy had no idea how to alert Rita, but at least she knew where she was.

# FIFTY-THREE

The sound of sirens echoed through the house, and everyone fell silent. Will confirmed then that the Barrister had indeed taken control of the local police and so had a veritable army out to destroy everything he'd missed in Montreal. A thought crossed his mind. He wondered how Franklin had escaped. He'd surely made a deal with the Barrister or had the whole thing planned all along. It dawned on Will that Franklin must have been the one to tell the Order about the meeting and the hurricane. He really was a traitor. There was no other explanation. Everyone who had been at that church was either dead or in this room. There was no time to think of all the angles. Things were crashing down around them too quickly.

Panic struck Franklin, but he controlled his facial expression quickly. Only a trained eye could note that he felt the serious peril they were suddenly in. The ancient enemy was outside and surely outmatched them in both number and firepower.

"We have to fight them off," he said with resignation in his voice.

"You brought this upon us, Sir Franklin," Will stated.

The old man cast a glare at him but then darted back to the door of the study.

"This way. Come on."

He pointed outside with his gun, and the two henchmen dutifully escorted Will and Dorothy while Franklin released Mr. Wilkinson's bonds. They all stood in the hallway, and from the large windows bordering the double doors ten patrol cars could be seen. It was a siege. Policemen were out with rifles, prepared for a firefight. From this angle, however, Will couldn't see the Barrister.

*He's out there somewhere.*

"Okay, Ben," Will said with sarcastic camaraderie. "Four soldiers, one near retirement, and two civilians against the entire Bermudan police force. That's a battle! Yeah! Bring them on!"

Will clapped his hands together in suicidal glee as Dorothy actually spat out a repressed chuckle.

"Shut the hell up!" Franklin barked, throwing the pistol in Will's face.

The old man was losing it. They were running out of options. This wasn't going according to his plan.

"Looks like going to the mob was the best decision I've made so far," said Will, now completely serious.

"I said, shut up!"

Will wasn't fazed. Although Franklin was losing control, he still needed Will to fight. He wouldn't shoot.

"So you were the one that tipped the Barrister off. Told the Society of Jesus exactly where the leaders of the heathens were meeting and why. All they had to do was show up and release the bullets, and in exchange, you were set free and pardoned by God. Is that it? Didn't think the son of a bitch would follow you all the way to Bermuda, did you?"

"I SAID SHUT UP!"

Franklin was serious this time. His gun was inches from Will's face, and panic showed in the older man's usually well-tempered features. His mind was slipping, and now Will wasn't so sure of his own safety. He'd have to stop his taunts or end up dead.

Movement caught his eye, and he backed up as subterfuge and cast a quick glance. To his concealed surprise, he caught sight of a young blonde girl, perhaps eighteen, coming out from a concealed door in the stairway and carrying a shotgun. He suddenly remembered that Dorothy had a sister. He had to keep up the charade or lose whatever advantage the girl had given them by coming in toward the group from behind.

He pressed on.

"You didn't count on Sammy messing up so much. Thought you'd have the key and the map and your man'd take care of me."

Will leaned in very close and whispered loudly enough to be heard by the room, "I don't have the key."

The old man's jaw dropped, and in that moment Will had enough time to seize control. He flew into action, thrusting his fist upward into Franklin's gut. The man keeled over with a surprised grunt, and Will snapped his wrist, making the gun drop into his free hand. In a skilled movement, he had Franklin under his arm, pistol placed to his head as the two goons, clearly shaken, pointed their guns desperately back at him. They then realized a shotgun was being pointed at them from behind. Having no other options, they lowered their weapons and backed away.

"You lost your focus," Will said to Franklin.

Dorothy immediately took action and grabbed the loose ropes from her father. As Will looked backward out the window, she tied the men up.

"You won't make it out of this," Franklin said, resigned to the situation.

"It's okay," Will said to the girl. "You can relax. Thank you."

She was very frightened. Glancing over at her sister and father, she slowly lowered the shotgun. Dorothy ran to her and after a hug and kiss, the young girl melted into a fit of weeping. Her father immediately came to her aid, and the three held each other, almost forgetting that Will had an active hostage.

A voice amplified by a megaphone sounded from outside.

"The house is surrounded!" it said. "Come out with your hands in the air and no one gets hurt!"

Franklin wasn't struggling, but the distance in his eyes suggested he was plotting. Will had very little time before this man turned the tables once more. Franklin was his mentor after all, and he undoubtedly knew techniques Will wasn't aware of. What was worse, Franklin knew everything Will did. His next move would have to be completely unexpected.

The silence in the room was deafening. The three civilians stood wide-eyed, still embracing but staring at Will for direction. The two goons were tied up and glaring. Franklin was subdued with a gun to his head and Will's arm around his neck.

"You have five seconds!" the megaphone shouted.

There was only one thing left to do.

"GO TO HELL, COPPERS!" Will suddenly shouted.

The others were stunned, but Dorothy managed to say, "What are you doing?"

"Get away from the door," he replied.

Will opened fire on the door, and in a single powerful gesture threw Franklin outside, diving out of the way. The next five seconds exploded in constant gunfire. The police unloaded on Franklin as he was cast out. Bullets ripped through the walls, shattered the windows, and split wood all up and down the staircase. The tied-up goons couldn't get out of the way, and one took several shots in the chest while the other lost his knee. Their howls sounded above the gunfire, along with shrieks from the Dorothy's sister.

Glancing around the corner of the study, Will saw that the civilians were safe inside, cowering.

"We don't have very much time," Will said. "How do we get out of here?"

Mr. Wilkinson pointed to the staircase from which Rita had emerged. Will noticed that he was now carrying the shotgun, much to the obvious relief of his youngest daughter.

"There's passage to the Crystal Cave through there. One cavern leads up to the surface. A very good friend of the family lives a quarter mile from there."

"That's our play, then," Will said. "Go ... go!"

The four of them poured into the hurricane shelter as the army of police outside reloaded and prepared to raid the house.

# FIFTY-FOUR

Nervously gripping his bare head in an attempt to maintain control, the Barrister watched as the pathetic excuse of a police force began their raid. A year ago this month, the police force owned a single bloody car. They had finally caught up after the introduction of the Motor Car Act. After counting quickly in his head, he realized that the ten vehicles at this house represented the entire Bermuda police fleet. He detested having to rely on locals for this, but he didn't have much time or very many options.

His own men needed to keep things secure in Montreal, and he'd already dispatched others to seek out the remaining Poor Fellow-Soldiers worldwide. He was down to only his personal crew of three men. His United Kingdom contacts came in handy, though, and he was able to mobilize the weak display of a police force in Bermuda before he'd landed a day and half prior. Fortunately, there had only been one major criminal investigation since the war, so the cops were quick and eager to respond. The Wilkinsons were very well known, and it had taken him all of half an hour to find out where Shakespeare was going.

He wasn't at all surprised to see Franklin run out like a mindless idiot, completely oblivious to the danger. Had he any smarts, he'd have accepted the deal and allowed God to do His work. Instead, greed had taken over, but that was always the case with heretics.

Money alone drove the bunch, and it had eventually driven them to this.

Heavy clouds began accumulating, and this heightened the Barrister's nerves. He kept neutral, so that only his personal crew knew something was wrong. Gripping his head was a habit not even thirty years of field combat experience could break. Two world wars, a half dozen revolutions, and countless violent regime changes in the armpits of the world, and he still couldn't help but grab his bald head when nervous.

He didn't want this operation to continue into the oncoming hurricane. A plane was ready at St. George's Naval Base, thanks to his contact at the newly established U.S. Department of Defense. They thought his operation was from the U.K. Ministry of Defence, and that's all they'd need to know. The problems in Berlin were putting the U.S. and U.K. directly into bed together against the U.S.S.R.; any civil dispute in a British colony would mean very little to the U.S., and in an effort to keep relationships strong, they would help without question.

Postwar life was going to be easier on the society than it had been before.

It wasn't the U.S. that was bothering him, nor was it the U.K. The police force was naïve and so opened fire on one enemy, making his job much easier. No questions would be asked, and in a few moments he'd finally put down Shakespeare and, sadly, the Wilkinson family, who'd got caught up in the nonsense. The mission was going like clockwork. What bothered him was God. Apparently, He'd decided to test the Barrister's faith by dispatching the largest hurricane the Caribbean had seen in over a hundred years directly in his path. He would curse, but he knew better. There was always a higher plan. In any case, the hurricane wouldn't hit for a couple of hours, or at least that's what he'd been told. They could fly out of the path to Cherry Point, North Carolina, where he'd enjoy a cocktail with some American G.I.s before returning to London.

He allowed the locals to secure the house. It took fifteen minutes, exactly twelve minutes longer than it would have had his own crew done the sweep. He finished his cigar and walked into the house only to find two bleeding and wounded men tied by the staircase. It confused him. These weren't the faces he'd expected to see.

"Where is the family?" he asked the police captain, a man named Bernes.

"No one here, sir, it is only these men."

"These men are enemies of the king."

Barely taking a moment to do it, he pulled out his pistol and casually killed both men with a single bullet each. Returning the gun to his shoulder holster, he looked around.

"There should be four others. Two men. One woman. One girl."

"Not here, sir," said the captain.

His voice quivered, and it annoyed the Barrister. Bernes wasn't used to ruthless acts of violence, perhaps, but there was absolutely no time to try to justify anything and certainly no time to smooth the action over. Thousands of years of history were riding on this, and he was stuck with gutless buffoons.

Glancing up, he noticed the stairway had a door, and it was closed.

"Did you check in there, Captain?"

"The closet? I'm sure a family could not ..."

"The United Kingdom spared your island from war, and now I can understand why."

The Barrister kicked the door open with little effort. Inside were mops, pails, brooms, linens ... and a steel hatch. He pointed at the hatch with feigned surprise and then put his cold face back on.

"Open the hatch, Captain, and send a team after the bastards."

"Yes, sir," he said, reddening in the cheeks.

"And, Captain, grow a bloody backbone before you completely exhaust me."

He'd send the cops in first and follow. The man they were hunting was very, very dangerous, and he wanted several human shields before reaching him. He'd exhaust Shakespeare with bodies, and then send his crew to finish the job. As he descended, his hands throbbed from his recent penance. He'd made a mistake killing that man on Oak Island, but there would be no more mistakes. The enemies of God would be put down this day.

# FIFTY-FIVE

The air was cold, but it didn't slow their pace at all. Panic and adrenaline did a good job of keeping them all together. Jogging through what seemed to be an endless unlit cavern, it was difficult to tell how far they'd gone before finally stopping. Dorothy knew they were stopping for supplies. Her father brought them to a side chamber that had been carved out by hand. A wooden closet was built inside holding rations, water canteens, and a dozen heavy black flashlights.

Passing everyone a light, her father said, "We'll follow this cavern as it veers right and opens up into a larger network of caves. Keep close to the wall and make sure you can always feel it on your left. After a few hundred meters, there will be a cavern we can follow to the surface."

As they started to head out, Dorothy's father pulled Will aside. Dorothy paused to listen.

"Sir William, your path is different. Go left here and don't stop until you reach the lake. You'll find a boat. Take it under the natural arch and then follow the map." He handed Will an ancient book. Will obviously objected to the instructions, but her father hushed him.

"Your mission is over. My daughter is safe now. Go."

Taking Dorothy's hand, her father brought her to the right, where they caught up with Rita. A ping of guilt stabbed at her as she felt the weight of the key on her hip. Was he going to try to get the treasure without the key? Was she prepared to concede this private battle? There wasn't any time to consider it, as she found herself in a sprint through the cavern and the comforting hand of her father in hers. Shakespeare was long gone, and she actually felt somewhat vacant. Something had been taken from her, and despite the guilt, she felt compelled to run away from it as fast as she could.

# FIFTY-SIX

Dank humidity bombarded the Barrister's senses as he descended from the hurricane shelter. It was impossible to see more than a meter ahead, so he gripped a nearby officer's flashlight and took it for himself, moving the officer behind him. Following the line of men as they went deeper in the cavern, he only looked backward to ensure his crew was nearby. They were close and taking lights for themselves.

He wanted to curse again. If this was a natural oceanic cavern, as he suspected it was, they could be anywhere. It would be very difficult to track them. His only consolation was that they were only minutes in front and that God was on his side. Straining to see in the dimness, he noticed an enclave to the side. Taking a sideward glance, he saw a pillaged supply closet.

They ascended to a series of chambers stretching forward and to the right. Jogging forward he caught up with the captain.

"Take a team to the right. Split up as necessary. I'm heading this way."

He took two of his men and sent the other two with the captain. Picking out four officers, he started into the larger cavern. It was not long before the walls receded enough in the distance to stop reflecting their light. He saw nothing but darkness ahead. They kept going quietly, but quickly, along the irregular rocky surface until they were suddenly met with a large underground lake stretching far into the darkness.

Stopping, the Barrister scanned the darkness. Nothing.

"Shut off your lights."

The men around him turned off the flashlights, and his vision went black. Allowing the images to dance away from his retinas, he closed his eyes. Opening them slowly he scanned the area again. He saw distant features ahead at the lake. Closing his eyes, he tried again. There was indeed an underground form, perhaps a stalactite or stalagmite. But it was barely distinguishable. In subterranean caverns, there was absolutely no source of light for eyes to adjust to. Seeing a feature across the lake meant only one thing. There was someone over there with a light .

"We need to get across this lake."

"Sir?"

"Get me a boat. A raft. Anything. Hurry!"

The officers snapped their lights on and jogged back toward the house.

"And get the others!" the Barrister barked after them.

# FIFTY-SEVEN

It was an impossible assignment, and Will knew it. Even as he paddled the four-man boat through the underground lake, he knew he was on a fool's errand. Without the key, he couldn't access the treasure. He knew better than to pursue it, but something inside him hoped he could get around it. It was highly doubtful considering the great lengths to which two generations of Drakes and some of the greatest engineering minds in history had gone to keep the Grail safe. There was no way he could simply walk in.

Impossible, perhaps, but necessary. Shakespeare allowed himself to go because he somehow believed it was going to work out, or he'd die trying. As the last able Poor Fellow-Soldier to fulfill his oath, he'd do everything in his power to rescue the wealth of human history out of treacherous clutches. He had no key, but he did have a map, and that was something that had never crossed his mind earlier.

The map to Drake's Harbor was perhaps as precious and elusive as the key. After Francis Drake had begun removing the treasure from Oak Island, he'd made a very thorough map of the Crystal Cave. It was the only map ever made of the complete cave system, and the Templars made sure of that. Many civilian lives had been lost at Templar hands to keep the secret safe. Francis Bacon completed his father's burden and bound it in a collection of his poems. The poems were actually poems designed to give the reader safe passage through

Drake's Harbor. If the book fell into the wrong hands and the poems couldn't be interpreted, death would surely take them before the treasure was found.

Unfortunately, Will wasn't high enough in the knighthood to know anything about the poems or what they meant. He couldn't even fathom how an authentic diary of Francis Bacon had ended up in the hands of the Wilkinsons. Will suspected the Wilkinsons were more than mere trusted civilians, but anyone at his level would know nothing more, and for good reason.

The only people who knew the true nature of this whole charade had died in Montreal, and the secret had died with them. If Will could make it past the gates and into Drake's Harbor, while interpreting the poems to help him avoid traps, he might be able to come closer to knowing what it was all about. Even then, he'd still have to figure out how to get the treasure to safety, and why, precisely, it was in danger. He feared that only Francis Bacon could know that.

He kept the flashlight low in the boat, offering only necessary light. Mr. Wilkinson's reference to the natural arch suddenly made sense. His boat was going through a massive forty-foot formation of stalactites and stalagmites that looked eerily like a gate into an abyss. Passing the connected arms of ancient stone, a sullen melancholy passed over him. This had to work out, but he had no idea how it would.

# FIFTY-EIGHT

Will pulled the rowboat onto the subterranean floor. It was slick and smooth, and so he struggled for a moment to keep traction. He cast the light into the cavern ahead and was very surprised to see an obvious set of stairs carved into the stone leading into a cavern. It was reminiscent of Oak Island, so he was sure it was the right way, but he was startled that it would be so obvious. Looking back, he realized the stretch across the lake was very far, and it was likely locals hadn't crossed it. Except, of course, for Mr. Wilkinson—for a civilian, he seemed to know quite a bit.

Before proceeding, Shakespeare looked at the map. It only took one page of the last part of the diary, and it was very simply laid out. A corridor stretched into an extremely large cavern where several buildings and docks had been built on a shoreline. Bacon had even marked where a dozen ships were placed at these docks, though Will doubted they still existed. There were easily thirty buildings inside Drake's Harbor, but the treasure wasn't marked in any of them. There were, however, numbers scrawled in various locations, as if marking important places. Double-checking to be sure, Will counted 154 of them altogether. There were too many places to look.

Absently flipping through the book, he noticed that a few lines sparked memories. Taking a closer look he realized that these weren't just poems. He bit his lips as he looked at them closer. His heart rate escalated.

They were William Shakespeare's sonnets.

Francis Bacon's sonnets were William Shakespeare's traditional 154 sonnets.

*Francis Bacon was William Shakespeare?*

Will blinked and thought for a moment about his name. Then he blinked again. Squinting, he knew time was short, so he set aside the realization.

The marks on the map referred to a sonnet in the book. William Shakespeare didn't write love poems ... it was Francis Bacon writing clues to find the Holy Grail.

It cast light on the whole mystery behind the sonnets. They were never meant to be published. When they were published in 1609, it likely created an uproar in the secret world, and it was clearly done without Bacon's approval. Most people thought William Shakespeare hadn't wanted his sonnets published, but this confirmed it.

Now, the problem. He had to read and decipher 154 Shakespearean sonnets to find the treasure. Admittedly, since taking on Shakespeare's name and completing his education in the knighthood, he was quite familiar with the work. Even still, he'd spent hardly any time on the sonnets, and it never occurred to him to do so. It wasn't the first thing one thought of when considering Shakespeare. In fact, many believed Shakespeare didn't even write the sonnets. Well, they were partially right. Bacon did.

Heaving a huge sigh, he decided to at least figure out what the first sonnet meant. He figured it must be the first sonnet, since the number "1" was scribbled into the entrance of Drake's Harbor, apparently right where he stood.

*From fairest creatures we desire increase,*
*That thereby beauty's Rose might never die,*
*But as the riper should by time decease,*
*His tender heir might bear his memory:*
*But thou, contracted to thine own bright eyes,*
*Feed'st thy light's flame with self-substantial fuel,*
*Making a famine where abundance lies,*
*Thyself thy foe, to thy sweet self too cruel.*

*Thou that art now the world's fresh ornament,*
*And only herald to the gaudy spring,*
*Within thine own bud buriest thy content,*
*And, tender churl, makest waste in niggarding.*
*Pity the world, or else this glutton be,*
*To eat the world's due, by the grave and thee.*

He may as well have been reading Greek. Trying again, he blinked and tried to clear his mind. The last two lines rang a bell. *Pity the world, or else this glutton be, / To eat the world's due, by the grave and thee.* It was a somewhat famous sonnet, and he recalled reading about it in one of the many Shakespeare texts he'd studied. Reading the poem again, he tried desperately to embrace the meaning. Recalling again the last line, it came back to him. He remembered an analysis of the sonnet that said it was about a young man who hadn't yet had a child. Apparently, Shakespeare was telling this man that he needed to have an heir so that his memory would be passed on.

Knowing now that the author of the sonnet was actually Francis Bacon, that meaning could hardly be right. Bacon had no children of his own and many male lovers. In fact, he detested the idea of royalty and the sanctity of marriage. His foster parents often had huge arguments with him on the subject. The thought that he'd written a sonnet suggesting that someone pass on an heir in order to preserve his memory seemed ridiculous. He read it again. Nothing.

Perhaps if he looked at the entrance to Drake's Harbor something would connect. Somewhat recklessly, Will jogged up the stairs and into the corridor. Normally he'd have taken his time and examined the area to make sure he wasn't being followed or that the hall wasn't blocked or a trap. There was no time for that. He knew he had precious minutes before the hurricane swells came, and being underground probably meant he'd get a front-row seat.

There was a simple door mounted into the wall of the cavern, and this startled him more than the stairs. Obviously made of sturdy oak and designed to handle almost any environmental concern, it was still surprising that the Templars had put their most prized possession behind a single door. Another thought occurred to him. If this was the only way in or out, how in the world would he manage to pull what would have to be an immense amount of treasure and documents through this small opening? Examining the door more closely, he saw that it was bolted so securely that not even a missile could get through. Utilizing the cavern around it, the door was lodged with several iron beams, presumably operated by the large and complex latch.

There was a keyhole on the latch.

Will cussed and sat down in frustration. He did need the key. Of course he did. That was the whole reason it had been put in Oak Island in the first place. Glancing upward, he saw some more construction above. More beams were lodged in the roof of the cavern. If the area was bombed out, those beams would fall, and it would be near impossible to get through. There had to be other such arrangements throughout the cavern, and, in fact, he wouldn't be surprised if the entire thing was handmade by Francis Drake and his men. It had taken two generations of men with near-unlimited resources to complete Drake's Harbor.

He pounded the door with the back of his head as he continued to explore the complete lack of options in front of him. Gripping the book, he gave the sonnet another read.

*From fairest creatures we desire increase,*
*That thereby beauty's Rose might never die*

He noticed that Bacon had capitalized the word "rose." In any other text in which he'd seen the poem, this, of course, wouldn't have been discernible. Likely, it wasn't even in the 1609 publication. "Rose" had a completely different meaning to the Order than to most of the world. It was a sort of slang or secret word they used to describe the Holy Grail. In fact, the mystic splinter group of the Templars and Masons, the Rosicrucians, had named their entire order after the word and concept—not after the Holy Grail itself but after the blossoming of ancient knowledge. That was the true meaning of the Holy Grail. It wasn't a cup of Christ; it was ancient knowledge. Surely that word had been chosen on purpose. In the new context, the first two lines came in a bit more clearly. As did the next two lines.

*But as the riper should by time decease,*
*His tender heir might bear his memory*

"Fairest creatures" were Templars or, more generally, those in the secret world. They didn't want the knowledge to be lost, but it could be lost over time. The only way to preserve it was to pass the knowledge down. Energy renewed in him, and he sat up and continued to read.

*But thou, contracted to thine own bright eyes,*
*Feed'st thy light's flame with self-substantial fuel,*

Because the Templars wanted the knowledge preserved so badly, they went to great lengths to ensure it was safe. But if they kept the knowledge "too" safe, they would have kept the knowledge away from the world completely. That would result in the same end the Templars were trying to avoid. The next two lines emphasized this thoughts:

*Making a famine where abundance lies,*
*Thyself thy foe, to thy sweet self too cruel*

That was absolutely what Bacon was saying. He was criticizing the Templars for wanting to keep the ancient knowledge secret. "Safe" was one thing; "secret" was another. Now the knowledge was completely meaningless. The very people the Templars were hoping to enlighten couldn't use it. They handicapped history by trying to protect it.

He kept reading.

*Thou that art now the world's fresh ornament,*
*And only herald to the gaudy spring,*
*Within thine own bud buriest thy content,*
*And, tender churl, makest waste in niggarding.*

He described the Templars as the only ones who could renew history. The most illuminated people on the planet, and instead of sharing their knowledge, they buried it, wasting the very value they held precious. The last lines were the clue as to how to proceed.

*Pity the world, or else this glutton be,*
*To eat the world's due, by the grave and thee.*

*Could it be? Was it possible?*
Will stood up in shock as the notion crossed his mind. Looking at the keyhole, he paused. Swallowing hard, he opened the latch, and after a heavy thud and a few iron knocks, the door creaked open for the first time in four hundred years. Will smiled as he realized the true meaning of Sonnet 1.

Francis Bacon didn't lock the door.

# FIFTY-NINE

Breaking through to the surface above the caverns was as much a relief as it was terrifying. Dorothy had no idea how much the storm had progressed. The wind had picked up; it was overcast, and rain was spattering onto the tropical forest around them. She could hear the distant sound of the road, which was normally not busy, but surely people were racing to shelter. She wondered very seriously how much time they had until the hurricane passed over them.

Seeing her father and sister in daylight calmed her nerves, but that only increased the guilt of the key weighing in her pocket. She couldn't go any farther, and her father immediately noticed.

"What is it? He can take care of himself."

She wanted to cry. Or scream. Or run away. Something. Anything. Instead she showed him the key, half knowing he'd understand exactly what it was.

"Why?" he asked in a whisper.

"I didn't know."

"I'll take it to him."

"No!" she shouted. There was no way she'd allow him to be in danger again.

"Please, Dorothy, you don't know the way."

"You'd never make it in time, Father. Tell me."

Resigning, he bowed his head. Coming back up with renewed confidence he said, "Go back the way we came, but keep along the wall. You'll eventually reach the lake. Follow it to the right until you reach a solid wall. You will need to swim, but not very far. You'll find the shore soon enough, and you can keep your hand on the wall through the lake if you need to. Keep going straight, and you'll see the stairs."

"Thank you," she said.

"Now promise me you'll give him the key and come straight back here. You know the way?"

She nodded and hugged him, then Rita. The heaviness brought her to tears, but she held them back. There was no time to be sentimental. Leaving her family behind, she went back into the cave as thunder clapped in the distance.

# SIXTY

onnet 2 made no sense at all. Will wiped an onslaught of sweat from his brow as he read. There was absolutely no time for this.

*When forty winters shall besiege thy brow,*
*And dig deep trenches in thy beauty's field,*
*Thy youth's proud livery, so gazed on now,*
*Will be a tatter'd weed, of small worth held:*
*Then being ask'd where all thy beauty lies,*
*Where all the treasure of thy lusty days,*
*To say, within thine own deep-sunken eyes,*
*Were an all-eating shame and thriftless praise.*
*How much more praise deserved thy beauty's use,*
*If thou couldst answer 'This fair child of mine*
*Shall sum my count and make my old excuse,'*
*Proving his beauty by succession thine!*
*This were to be new made when thou art old,*
*And see thy blood warm when thou feel'st it cold.*

The map marked "2" at the end of the passageway he'd just entered. It formed the mouth of the main cavern and the opening to Drake's Harbor. Will's heart raced as he realized how close he was. Thinking back on the first sonnet, he didn't rush forward. It had set up not only a way in but also a trap. Had he used the key, he'd have been the "glutton" trying to keep the treasure secret still, and there was a clear "grave" reference. Will had no doubt that turning the key on that latch would have destroyed the entire chamber, perhaps by flooding or simply by collapsing the walls. In any case, he had to proceed carefully.

According to this sonnet, there was a way through and also a trap. Reading it again, he tried to pull himself back and apply the words strictly to the situation. Running them through his mind meant nothing. Clearly, before he could investigate any of the other locations in Drake's Harbor, he would have to get past this one.

The first four lines were merely describing the treasure or perhaps the harbor. That at the time it was built, it looked perfect, but over time it would decay. That was obvious enough, but what was the point? Then the next part jumped off the page.

Of course! The next thing he'd want to know was where the treasure was, but no one alive could tell him.

> *Then being ask'd where all thy beauty lies,*
> *Where all the treasure of thy lusty days,*
> *To say, within thine own deep-sunken eyes,*
> *Were an all-eating shame and thriftless praise.*

The next part would have the clue.

Was he suggesting that something inside would tell him the location? Something was intentionally left behind? He read the lines aloud: "This fair child of mine ... Proving his beauty by succession thine." That was what he was looking for, but how? "And see thy blood warm when thou feel'st it cold."

Stumped. Was he supposed to turn on the lights? Will looked farther into the darkness ahead. Creeping very slowly, he went forward up to the point marked on the map. Sure enough, a vacant coolness pounded back at him as he emerged and the walls disappeared on either side of him. He was at the mouth of Drake's Harbor. Looking once again at the sonnet, he studied the last few lines.

Maybe he needed a torch.

Will looked to his left and saw a wooden duct built into the chamber wall. A black liquid settled inside, and it seemed to stretch far into the cavern, no wider or deeper than a few inches. Very carefully he went over and stuck his finger inside. Taking a small whiff, he realized it was lamp oil. Maybe he was supposed to turn on the lights. But what was the trap?

Looking over the sonnet again, it was the last line that stuck with him because that was the line that had the trap in the first sonnet. "And see thy blood warm when thou feel'st it cold." It still meant nothing. Was he supposed to be cold when he did it? Will looked on the other side. The walk sloped downward into another underground lake. Looking back toward the harbor, there appeared to be a bridge ahead. Throwing his light around, he suddenly noticed another duct a foot or so above the water along the chamber wall.

That has to be it.

Checking his lighter and at the same time moving his cigarettes to his breast pocket, Will slipped into the water. Surprisingly it was quite cold. More sure than ever of the meaning, he continued forward. Now submerged up to his neck, he rolled his eyes at the fact that he got his cigarettes wet anyway. Falling into the water, he reached up and placed the flame of his lighter into the duct.

# SIXTY-TWO

Drake's Harbor suddenly flared up into complete illumination. The oil duct threw a wall of fire into the air that circled all the way through the chamber, splitting off into other ducts suspended high above and going too far in the distance to measure. The first thing he realized was that he was looking up at an actual underground medieval city. The second thing he saw was a fleet of twelve perfectly intact carrack ships at dock in the city, their sails and flags all in full suspension high above the harbor. His breath left him.

*No wonder it had taken two generations.*

Taking his fedora off in respect and homage for his senior Templars, Will crept back onto the shore, where he had an impressive view over the whole place. Streets, houses, taverns, docks, even a strip full of merchant tents. It was a fully functional port town all built to support the breathtaking fleet of ships at her docks.

Then at once the second sonnet made sense. The largest and most impressive ship sat in the center of the docks, and on its sail was painted the distinctive red Templar cross. All the other ships carried no symbology except for the Jolly Roger. None but those with the wealth f Drake, Elizabeth and Bacon could have created such a paradise.

It was very difficult to believe that it had lasted nearly a thousand years, but there it was, just as they had sat in the days of Bacon, of Drake before him, and of Sinclair before them. Drake's Harbor was a masterpiece of engineering, everything delicately put into its place and dramatically illuminated by rivers of fire suspended high above the cavern.

He had no idea how long he stood there, stunned like an animal in shock. Trying to shake the vision away, he turned his attention back to the diary. Then a question hit him. Jogging over to the other duct, he saw it wasn't lit. Following the duct's path, he realized in silent horror that it led to the docks. Had he lit it, the ships would have gone up in flames.

*This place has more traps than a speakeasy.*

The impressive wooden bridge that stood before him led into the main path of Drake's Harbor: a cobblestone street leading directly to the docks. The merchant tents were set up along this stretch along with the highest buildings, some reaching four stories. They were all long ago abandoned, but there seemed to be every possible sundry and luxury one could think of. Will could spot barrels of rum and water, chests of spices, and other various containers and vessels all along the streets. Inside he could see the shadows of furniture and chandeliers. Historic statues were planted in courtyards along with pillars and even a few obelisks.

The Templar treasure was everywhere. It had been placed in all these buildings to decorate the secret city. Thousands of years' of wealth from Asia, the Middle East, and Europe were all here in a private and elaborate storage closet. Glancing back at the diary, he realized there must be 152 actual deposits of treasure, and each one was equally accessible or trapped depending on the corresponding sonnet. It would take years to figure it all out.

He had minutes.

Fortunately, Francis Drake knew the real reason a traveler would come here. There was only one treasure important enough to risk everything to get. It wasn't gold, pearls, statues, or gems. It was far more precious than that. Sonnet 2 told Will that when the lights were on, he would know where the Grail was. And he did. It was on the ship with the Templar's cross. He looked at the map, and it was confirmed. The ship was marked as 13—the Templar's most sacred number. The perfect choice for Bacon to place the Holy Grail.

Will found Sonnet 13 and read:

*O, that you were your self! but, love, you are*
*No longer yours, than you your self here live:*
*Against this coming end you should prepare,*
*And your sweet semblance to some other give:*
*So should that beauty which you hold in lease*
*Find no determination; then you were*
*Yourself again after yourself's decease,*
*When your sweet issue your sweet form should bear.*
*Who lets so fair a house fall to decay,*
*Which husbandry in honour might uphold*
*Against the stormy gusts of winter's day*
*And barren rage of death's eternal cold?*
*O, none but unthrifts! Dear my love, you know*
*You had a father: let your son say so.*

It seemed to say so much. Bacon was being very personal, and if Will didn't know better, this sonnet was written to Francis Drake—perhaps a final homage to their projects and separate lives. He named the place Drake's Harbor and obviously felt an obligation to finish his true father's legacy. There was no doubt Bacon would have wanted to announce his true lineage to the world. He was likely very proud of his father and wanted to pass on his honor. Did he perhaps hold resentment for the Templars or the Grail itself for keeping his father and the Queen anonymous?

It couldn't be only that. There was a message in Sonnet 13 that kept the Holy Grail preserved while avoiding a very tragic trap. It would be the most elusive of them all. It had to be. This would be the most difficult puzzle. This was the prize of all men and the ultimate secret. It was the whole reason Sinclair had launched a mission to the New World and built Oak Island, and it was the very reason that Francis Drake plundered Oak Island and began work on Drake's Harbor. It was also the reason Francis Bacon had finished the job and made such an elaborate scheme to ensure its safety or its destruction should the secret be violated.

The Templars wanted to protect the secret so badly they would destroy it rather than release it. Will was beginning to believe that

Bacon resented that as well. His sonnets were equally practical and emotional. He was telling his story through them and in doing so was addressing a much bigger picture than his own life. Perhaps the William Shakespeare identity itself was a way of broadcasting his true life to the world. If Will ever made it out of here alive, he would read each play with a great deal of scrutiny.

In the meantime, he had to decipher Sonnet 13. It was even more enigmatic than the others. There must be a way. He'd begin a walk to the ship holding the Holy Grail, stepping foot on the very soil that Bacon and Drake had walked on. There could be no mistakes.

Then he heard a sound behind him as a rock tumbled into water. Twirling on his heels, he let out a sigh of relief when he saw Dorothy standing there.

"Miss Wilkinson, you scared me."

Her eyes were distant. Fearful. He recoiled, but it was too late. The bald head of the Barrister poked in from the darkness, and before looking around he said, "You shouldn't stray from the path of God; He may send a natural disaster."

# SIXTY-THREE

There were three policemen and two of his crew, Sir Thomas and Sir William. The Barrister knew he had his prey. Now he could just sit back and watch the events unfold in leisure. He gently prodded the woman with his pistol, and she stumbled down to her criminal boyfriend, who took her and feigned a comforting embrace. Behind him was an awesome sight, an underground city complete with ships.

"So this is where you've been hiding relics from the Church."

"Protecting them," Shakespeare stated.

The Barrister didn't even award that comment a response. If the crusaders did in fact hold the Holy Grail, or the Ark of the Covenant, these things clearly belonged to the Church that Christ founded and not to a bunch of heathens—sodomizing heathens. If they had their way, the world would be back in Rome worshipping ridiculous statues of naked men. These were civilized times now. There was no room for these archaic knighthoods. The Barrister would end it tonight.

The ship with the red cross caught his eye, and behind it, a stream of water was leaking from the cavern walls. It had begun. God's wrath would soon be revealed. That ship remained in his sight. Suddenly it dawned on the Barrister like a divine light. God spoke to him. This was it! This was why God had sent him into the bowels of the hurricane. It would be the only way the crusaders would hand over the Holy Grail.

He was there to do God's will. He would take back what belonged to God—not destroy it. If God wanted it destroyed, they never would have gone through this whole charade. It all suddenly made sense.

"I'll make this simple," he said as calmly as he could. He raised the pistol directly to Dorothy's head. "Give me the Holy Grail, and I'll let Miss Wilkinson live."

Will's eyes darkened.

A stone fell far in the distance into the harbor. It was a signal.

"There is not much time. The swell will completely fill this chamber. Destroy everything you've been trying to protect. Give that protection to the Church, and the civilian lives. Refuse, you all die and I'll take it myself."

The Bermudans whispered behind him. The Barrister turned and shot all four of them one by one before turning his pistol back to Dorothy.

The color drained from her face, and her eyes were wide with terror. Shakespeare remained calm.

The Barrister still had his crew, and the last thing he needed were some bumbling idiots screwing it all up, getting a conscience, or worse, fleeing the caves with stories about the Holy Grail.

"Where were we? Oh, yes. The Grail."

"I don't know how to get it," Shakespeare said.

Of course he was lying, but how much more serious could he make the proposition?

"There isn't time for this, Poor Knight."

"It's a riddle," Will said and handed a book over.

The Barrister looked down, saw a poem, and threw it back.

"Poetry?"

"If you don't have the patience to hear what is going on here, then you'll kill us and never get the Grail. In fact, Drake's Harbor will kill you if you try. I am the only one who can figure this out."

If it was a bluff, it was a good one. Somehow, the bastard had managed to turn the tables on him. He didn't have much to lose on this arrangement, and if Shakespeare was stalling, they'd find out soon enough.

"Very well. Figure it out."

# SIXTY-FOUR

Those words stung. Will pulled Dorothy close and offered as much comfort as he could, but the thought of figuring out Sonnet 13 with all the time in the world was daunting enough. Now he was under gunpoint with a hurricane flooding the cavern. He picked up the book and scanned the verses again. Nothing clicked.

He would have to see the ship.

Leading them all into the town, he desperately wished he could take more time and explore this phenomenon. History wouldn't have it. He would only be able to go after the prize. Drake's Harbor was only two hundred yards long, at best, but their walk seemed to take an eternity. Occasionally stones would fall into the harbor beyond. Will hoped that didn't mean they were now under the ocean and the walls were collapsing from the weight.

Finally arriving at the ship, Will almost forgot the situation. Looking at its glorious craftsmanship and ancient splendor, he was momentarily stunned. It looked to be in pristine condition and carried the very flags that Sir Francis Drake had put there. These were perhaps the same ships that Sinclair had used four hundred years before Drake. It was curious to note that although each was anchored, there was a network of ropes connecting them.

Hesitant but seeing no other option, Will started up the plank to the deck of the Templar ship. With each step he felt the weight of his nerves increase. He didn't fully understand the sonnet and could easily set off a trap simply by boarding the ship. He had no direction and hoped that by seeing the deck, the words would make sense. All the while he tried to ignore the Barrister and his men and kept Dorothy's hand tightly in his.

So much for his mission.

*O, that you were your self! but, love, you are*
*No longer yours, than you yourself here live*

"I am not myself. I am no longer in control of myself," he interpreted.

*Against this coming end you should prepare,*
*And your sweet semblance to some other give:*
*So should that beauty which you hold in lease*

"There is an end that I should prepare for. I should give someone else sweetness so that the beauty I hide can be shown."

*Find no determination; then you were*
*Yourself again after yourself's decease*

"I should not be determined, but be myself again as if I were dead."

He tapped the book and then said thoughtfully, "Then my beauty is genuine. Then those who have decaying homes but honorable names withstand storms, anger, and death. But it is all unnecessary."

And then he read the last line: "You had a father: let your son say so."

It was a letter from Bacon to Drake. It had to be. Bacon felt incomplete and would not reveal his true nature without giving back what his father had hidden from him. And his intention was quite clear. Unlocking the Holy Grail would release the secret upon the world. By getting the treasure, these ships would set sail.

He looked around suddenly into the darkness.

"But where to?" he said aloud.

The Barrister immediately reacted. Will had almost forgotten he was there.

"What is it?"

Will then realized that the Barrister wasn't talking to him.

# SIXTY-FIVE

Will wandered off deep in thought. Dorothy suspected he'd been challenged a great deal since going into Drake's Harbor. Now seeing it firsthand, she wasn't only a true believer; she felt the pressure of her old life and actions. She had to do everything she could to make sure this mission did not fail. It seemed hopeless, but it didn't matter. She owed it to Shakespeare.

The Barrister was clearly preoccupied with Will as he paced the deck, listening to him speak eclectic phrases, pondering over words. She took the opportunity to take a close look at the ship. The rigging was definitely old, but it was remarkable how intact the ship was. It was almost as if someone had been caring for it all these years. Just as the thought crossed her mind, she realized that it must have been her father. Everything fell into place. He was the caretaker, and he always had been. And perhaps her grandfather before him. How long had this been going on?

Brushing it all aside, she focused, and in so doing, she saw the reason she was there. By the time she realized it, the Barrister noticed she'd wandered off. Instead of paying any attention to him, she turned to Will.

"I've kept something from you."

Will walked closer to her with a furrowed brow. She'd become used to his neutral expression and seeing the hint of emotion caught her off guard. Rather than prolonging the moment, she pulled the key from her pocket. Will nearly lost his balance. Staring at her with complete shock, he reluctantly took it. Then he saw what she saw.

The door to the hold had an ornate single keyhole in its center.

# SIXTY-SIX

*S*he had the key.

Will was stunned. Military instincts took over, and he crushed the implications of her actions as quickly as possible. The sonnet was clear. This was it. Gripping the key, he turned to the Barrister as if he was a member of his unit.

"If I unlock this door, we will find the Holy Grail, but then these ships will set sail."

The Barrister chuckled but stopped as he realized that Will was serious.

"Where will they go?"

"That's the chance we have to take by getting the prize. You have the gun, Barrister, so I'm leaving the choice up to you."

The bald man took a step backward, staring at Will with open shock. He looked at the door and then back to Will.

"This is a trick."

"No trick, Barrister. I just want you to know what you're getting into."

A large rock crashed into the water behind them. Everyone, including the Barrister's crew, squinted in the darkness to see it. They were out of time. The hurricane had come.

"Do it," the Barrister said quietly.

Will slowly walked over to the hold door. Placing the key in the lock, he turned it. A quiet latch sounded and then nothing.

The silence didn't last long enough for anyone to respond.

The anchors of all twelve ships began rising at once with clattering mayhem. The sound of hidden wheels and sprockets echoed throughout the cavern, and a horrifyingly familiar thud resonated from deep inside the water.

Will suddenly got it.

*It's another Oak Island.*

"Hold on!" he barked, and no one hesitated.

The ship suddenly shifted, and with impossible speed spun around toward the dark harbor. Before long, it was shifting again, the other ships ahead of it in single file, all attached by a network of ropes. The ship changed course again, and it became obvious that they were going around in circles.

"What's happening?" the Barrister shouted above the increasingly loud pounding of the waves around them.

"The harbor is draining!" Will shouted back.

"What?"

"DRAINING!"

But as he dictated the events around them, it all became clearer. The water level was dropping so quickly, the cavern's walls seemed to be rising around them. In only a few moments, the walls stretched far enough into the darkness that they could no longer see the fire-lit city. The ship jerked, yawed, and rocked violently as it followed the path of the massive harbor-sized vortex.

Will took the time to try to illuminate the deck. Taking his lighter to various lanterns on the ship, he was able to make more sense of their surroundings. The ship's lights reflected off the walls in serene but spooky brilliance, making ghostly shadows of the other ships ahead of them.

Then an opening appeared in one of the walls. That's when Will started to figure it out. It really was like Oak Island. This chamber was draining into another one, allowing the water to go low enough so that the ships could go through a passageway built under the harbor. The question was where it would bring them out.

Sure enough, the cavern opened up completely, and the ships all barreled inside, taken in by the swift current below them. They crashed through wakes, launching all over the deck. Will noticed that Dorothy was clutching on to him. Squinting through the dim light, he hoped they would soon arrive at their destination.

He thought he was going to be sick.

The corridor opened up around them, and he was stunned to see daylight ahead. As they approached, it became even more brilliant until the ships rushed out into a rather turbulent bay surrounded by hundreds of feet of rock. Rain exploded around them, and gusts of wind whipped down into the crater. The hurricane was upon them.

"Where is this?" Dorothy asked.

Will shrugged—he wasn't the Bermudan. The ships fell into a somewhat placid state, rocking around each other in an odd flock-like formation. The Barrister took the opportunity to assert his authority.

"Open the hold!"

Will did. He was just as excited to see what his life was all about. Quickly going inside, he let his eyes adjust. What he saw caused him to fall to his knees.

This was it. This was the moment. God would finally have His prize safe with its rightful owners. The Barrister's work would strengthen the Church beyond measure. He had done God's work. Everything he'd done in his civilian life and the wars he'd fought would finally be worth it. Peering from behind Shakespeare, he couldn't see what had made him drop.

Surely it was the beauty of it all.

"It's not here," Will said barely above a whisper.

The Barrister nearly shot him but held back. His anger had to be controlled. He needed this bastard for now. Biting his knuckle, he took a deep breath.

"Then, Sir William. Where is it?"

"This was the trap. I don't know!"

The Barrister grabbed the woman and once again placed a gun to her head.

"Find it!" he ordered.

The ship lurched suddenly, and the Barrister's heart leapt as he saw the gun fly from his fingers. There was no time to gather it because the ship was in another vortex current, being dragged forward at high speed. Waves crashed over the side, and he saw that whatever hole they were in was being filled with water. The process was reversing itself.

Shakespeare had to be lying. If it were a trap, the ships wouldn't be set free safely. The woman took advantage of the situation and wrenched free of the Barrister's grasp, but he was still within arm's reach of the gun. Jumping forward, he fell close, but not close enough. Shakespeare kicked him heavily in the gut.

The Barrister's crew was mobilized, and he saw them jump into action. Gunfire resounded, and he sat up, certain Shakespeare was down.

He wasn't.

The ship yawed violently, and Will lost his footing. The Barrister regained his balance long enough to see if Shakespeare had shot both his men. He had. One was reeling from an abdomen shot, and the other had been hit in the head.

Shakespeare rolled to take a shot at the Barrister but fell backward on another one of the ship's lunges. The momentum tossed the gun into the ocean.

He was going to put an end to this. A quick glance around the deck showed him there was a weapon within his grasp.

# SIXTY-SEVEN

Dorothy was beyond fear now, and adrenaline took over. She scrambled to kick the guns away from the men Shakespeare had shot. Even seeing the man's head wound didn't faze her much. Making sure they were safe, she looked back to see where Shakespeare was. He was regaining his balance but was suddenly taken off guard as the Barrister charged him with a sword.

Looking downward, Dorothy saw a whole rack of swords within arm's reach. Quickly grabbing one, she shouted Will's name and tossed him one. He blocked the Barrister's charge at the very last second but wasn't prepared for the blow, falling hard on his back. The Barrister took another swing. Will rolled out of the way and then jumped to his feet.

Dorothy grabbed another sword for herself and then noticed that the walls were disappearing around them; they were in Harrington Sound. In a stunned moment, she realized that the trap had completely drained Bermuda's Harrington Sound. She couldn't reflect on it very long because the full strength of the hurricane dropped on top of them.

Standing on a bucking ship was difficult enough, but avoiding an oncoming sword in seventy-five-mile-an-hour wind on a ship was quite impossible. Will tumbled backward and managed to get to his feet in time to meet the Barrister's swordplay. Not quite believing he was actually involved in a swordfight, it took several parries of very aggressive overhead strikes before he began to manage the feel of the combat style.

Two consecutive overhead strikes and three side strikes forced Will's fined-tuned ability right away. The wind threw pellets of water dangerously into his face, forcing him to adjust his balance. Just as he'd find the right footing, the ship would yaw and knock him back a few steps. Fortunately, the Barrister was confronting the same conditions.

Finally getting the hang of the combat, Will pressed forward with his own attacks, bringing the Barrister into a series of parries. Just as Will overcame him, the ship yawed again, and this time the climb was so high and the drop so low that everyone on the deck came crashing down, followed by some cases and barrels that were loosely arranged under corroded rope.

Taking the opportunity to look at their surroundings, Will saw that the other ships were pulling out of the sound and into the open ocean. The waves would easily be going from ten feet to a thirty-foot swell. Groaning only enough to display his frustration at the situation, he climbed back to his feet to meet the Barrister once more in swordplay.

They scattered their efforts all across the deck, and as he passed her, Will noticed Dorothy had a sword of her own. He sincerely hoped she wouldn't try to step in. The Barrister would easily cut her open. The trepidation on her face suggested she wasn't quite prepared to do so.

The winds were intolerable now, and the closer they got to the ocean, the worse it became. Will used every means he could to conserve energy, but the Barrister was coming on very strongly. Somewhat surprised at his strength and skill, Will fought merely to keep up. As the blows came down heavier and heavier, he realized his strength was waning. Taking strikes from above and to the side, he kept his ancient sword in a steady defensive position, doing nothing but stopping the Barrister's blade.

To Will's horror, Dorothy then charged forward. Screaming, she brought her sword high, giving the Barrister plenty of opportunity to respond by doing so. He simply spun on his heel and threw a high kick directly into her face. A trail of blood jumped out of her nose, and she fell firmly on the deck. Even with the kick, he was able to repel Will's feeble counterattack.

Dorothy was undoubtedly unconscious. It was just the two of them now. Exhaustion was taking over, and Will was sure it was written all over his face. Despite the wind, rain, and oncoming waves, the Barrister remained expressionless. There was no guessing who had the upper hand.

Then they broke through the sound and crashed into the ocean. A wall of water surmounted the bow and drove the boat downward in a sudden and vertical lurch. The deck crashed and tumbled as both men lost their footing and fell hard into the wall of the cabin. Buoyancy still reigned, and the ship exploded out of the swell, the bow launching high above the crashing waves. Settling back into the sea, waves pounded both sides of the ship as the water level fell. Another lurch, and the ship rocked in heavy resonance against the persistent waves. Now high on the swell, a steady wash came over the side.

At least the chaos was somewhat orderly now, and Will could stand once again. The winds were far worse than in the sound, and he found it difficult to keep on his feet without gripping the rigging or the rails. Still keeping his sword in one hand, he squinted through the pelting horizontal rain for his nemesis.

Like a shadow in fog, the Barrister charged forward, his sword held high with two hands. He brought the blade crashing down.

Will knew he wasn't prepared but attempted to block the powerful blow. He managed to keep the blade from cutting him in two, but the momentum knocked him several yards backward, and his sword flew far into the storm.

It was over. He'd failed. Trying to stand, he found his legs weakened from the crash, and he fell back over. Sensing the steps of the Barrister above him, Will whispered, "So mote it be."

But it didn't happen. A surprised grunt spat out above the sound of the waves around them. Will looked up and saw a sword running through the Barrister, directly under his sternum. His eyes were wide, and bloody saliva was leaking onto his chin. Behind him was Dorothy, holding the hilt of the sword with all her might.

The Barrister collapsed to his knees, life draining quickly. She surely hadn't aimed, but Will was certain his lungs had collapsed. The man had seconds to live.

Looking blankly at Will as he crumpled over, he said, "I don't understand ..."

Wondering if he was talking to him, Will cocked his head and watched the dying man more closely. At the moment of his last breath, he gripped the rosary around his neck. He was talking to God.

Dorothy fell down next to Will and embraced him. Despite her determined eyes, she was crying. This civilian had seen enough death to last a lifetime, and now she'd saved his life. The hurricane roared around them, but for a few precious seconds, Will heard and felt nothing but the woman next to him.

Strength began to return, and he stepped away from the embrace. Standing against the wind, he looked out over the deck. The ships were pulling them deeper into the ocean and through the storm; he'd lost sight of Bermuda altogether.

"The Grail isn't here," he shouted above the wind.

Squinting once more, he saw the answer. The ship ahead of them held a flag with the traditional Masonic square and compass symbol. It was clearly a Masonic flag of the Scottish Rite. The sonnet came back to him. "You had a father: let your son say so." The Masons were born from the Templars. He cursed Bacon's name under his breath. He'd put the Holy Grail under the Masonic flag, not the Templars'. It was another gesture of his desire for the Templars to recognize their true past. He wanted the Masons to no longer be separate, uniting the strongest fraternities in the world. He'd given the treasure to the Masons.

"It's there!" Will shouted, pointing.

The currents were whipping the ship through this swell and probably into another. They would go farther and farther out to sea until they met the eye, and the eye wall would sink them all. He was on the wrong ship, and his mission lay elsewhere.

Jumping down to the Barrister's corpse, Will pulled out the sword. Climbing to the bow, he ignored Dorothy's shouts behind him and reached dangerously over the side.

The ship yawed downward, but he kept a firm grip on the rail. With two very strong swipes, he cut the rigging tying them to the other ships. The Templar ship was now free. He had to get it back to the sound, the only place it would be safe, but he knew as much about sailing as he did about theoretical mathematics. Looking up at the sails, he saw them torn and blown out from the winds.

"We need to get back to the sound," he shouted above the wind.

Dorothy pointed behind her to a higher deck at the stern.

"The wheel! We have to turn around!"

Just then a wave crashed over the side and sent them both spinning to opposite sides of the deck.

"Will!" she shouted.

Will crawled back over to her.

"I am not your mission anymore!"

"What?"

"I AM NOT YOUR MISSION!"

The wind was deafening, but he heard her clearly.

She continued her shouting. "Go get the Grail! I can take the ship home!"

That was ludicrous on many levels.

"It's the Holy Goddamned Grail!" she persisted. "I'll be fine! I've sailed my whole life!"

*Has she sailed fourteenth-century carracks?*

Her eyes were serious.

"GO!" she yelled.

He didn't know if she was right or wrong, but the overwhelming urge to save humankind's most ancient knowledge took over. Perhaps it was adrenaline or outright stupidity, but he silently agreed, refusing to allow himself to think about it. In an unexpected gesture, he grabbed Dorothy's face with both hands and kissed her long enough for her to know he meant it.

"Don't wait up for me," he said and ran over to the end of the deck, where he removed his shoes, jacket, and tie and then jumped over the side.

# SIXTY-EIGHT

The kiss wasn't completely unexpected. It was very possible Shakespeare was going to his death. It took very little incentive for Dorothy to stop watching him as he went overboard. Waves continued to pound the ancient deck, and the swell was going nowhere. She scrambled to her feet and climbed to the deck despite the wind. The wheel was spinning almost uncontrollably. She grabbed the handles, and the momentum nearly threw her down. With all of her might, she wrestled it under control and held it steady. She spun the wheel hard over; she needed to move the ship into a dangerous U-turn.

The keel creaked loudly, even penetrating the sound of the storm around her. As expected, the ship listed starboard, and it seemed as if the ocean was completely swallowing the deck. The fear of capsizing was forefront in her mind as waves continued to plunge onto the deck. Her stomach bottomed out, leaving vacant and frozen terror. There was no real certain way to know if the turn was sufficient, as landmarks were long gone. She scanned the stormy horizon for any indication and was overwhelmed with relief when she saw the faint glow of the Flatts Village on the only entry point into Harrington Sound.

A turn was still needed but not hard over. Quickly spinning the wheel back, the deck popped out from under the wave caps. The swell still sloshed heavily on the deck, but it wasn't completely submerged. At last, the lights fell into line, and she let the wheel spin back. The worst was over, and the sound would save this ship. She was stunned the craft was still operational; not even the hurricane winds could dampen the determination welling up inside her.

The ship screamed and creaked as she adjusted the wheel. Winds tore through the sails, but enough remained to keep her cutting through the swell. Valleys sent the bow deep, but it climbed the crests with valiance. The small peaks around the sound came into view, and to her relief the ship was marching straight through the Flatts Inlet. The winds were already dying down.

Dropping down from the swell was terrifying. The ship crashed through a wall of water, and a profound creak echoed around her. The blast knocked her over, and the wheel spun from her clutches. Crashing echoed around her, and she saw the front mast toppling over onto the deck, the rigging snapping away in the rain.

The ship spun out of her control and drifted sideways into the sound, but the smaller waves relieved the creaks of the hull. She stood up and steered the ship back on course across the sound. Although certainly violent, it wasn't as bad as the swell. Using the last of her strength, she released the anchor and crawled into the captain's cabin.

# SIXTY-NINE

The power of the world took grip of Will's entire body as he fell into the hurricane swell. No longer a victim of high winds, he was now being tossed into twenty-foot peaks and valleys. Wave caps crashed over him, and although he'd jumped in knowing he was ill prepared, he'd very much underestimated the situation.

Only able to spot the ships at the peaks of the waves, he paddled quickly, spitting out lungfuls of water and then treading water when tumbling into a valley. Fortunately, no waves were breaking over him at the moment, but peering into the rocky madness of the seascape ahead of him, he knew it was only a matter of time. Hoping he was being carried by the same current as the fleet, he continued to swim in the ever-darkening waters.

Cresting another huge wave, his arms started going numb. It didn't matter how athletic he was; very soon he'd run out of strength. Already spent from the fight aboard the ship, he was now swimming in hurricane waters. The wave cast him into a valley, and he saw above him the stern of the Masonic ship rising from the water like a monolith. His goal in sight, he swam with a new burst of adrenaline. At last he found the cut rigging, trailing the ship from far behind. He grabbed it with both hands and climbed forward toward the ship.

It looked like a wooden monster, rocking unpredictably in the swell. The closer he got, the more it seemed like it would just suck him under. With arms like rubber and near-empty lungs, he desperately climbed forward. At last, he gripped the ancient and slippery hull with both hands, letting the ship snag him out of the water. Taking a few breaths and spitting out the ocean, he gripped the ship tight and circled it, looking for loose rigging.

Ten feet of breaking water towered over him, and he braced himself. It was as if he'd been dropped from a three-story building. His body jolted and tumbled. Flying aimlessly beneath the water, he was jerked into turbulent currents. When it passed, his lungs ached, but he wasn't hurt. Scrambling back to the surface, he saw the Masonic ship at a distance. The wave had sent him back to where he'd started.

Another wave hit Will from behind, and he swam with it, just keeping ahead of the drop. Fortunately, this six-footer was small enough to ride. Stiffening his body, Will let the wave carry him to the ship, and a sight in the water rewarded his earnest plight. He found the cut rigging again and grabbed it before the six-footer's undertow brought him back, he felt the force of the Masonic ship tug him forward.

Ignoring his failing arms and aching limbs, the burning lungs and the running sinuses, he grabbed the rope with all his strength. Taking it one arm length at a time, he pulled himself forward as waves tossed him to and fro. He finally reached the hull again, but this time it was far less daunting. Heaving himself up the side, another wave crashed over him, but this one tossed him up onto the deck. Floundering in sprawling mayhem, he slapped around on the ship like a landed fish.

Regaining his balance, Will lay silent and rested on the deck as waves splashed around him. Howling winds ripped above him, and the familiar groans and creaks of a strained keel reverberated below. He looked up when the ship violently lurched forward. The earsplitting sound of a hull splitting crackled through the wind-worn air. Unable to see the source, Will managed to stand. Braced against the side of the ship, he peered through the storm.

The ship ahead of him had capsized. Massive masts cracked from the weight, and the hull was breaking not far from the bow. A wave crashed on top of it and completely took it over, throwing a thunderous groan above the storm. A panicked thought hit him as he realized that the sinking ship was tied to his own.

Slipping across the deck, he scrambled for a weapons' closet.

They weren't as accessible as they were on the Templar ship—at least not in sight, anyway.

He tried the captain's cabin, but the door was jammed. Pounding it with his shoulder was like hitting a cinderblock wall. The ship lurched again and threw him backward toward the bow. To his horror, he saw the ship being pulled downward. Running out of options, he tried kicking the door. It creaked. Ramming it with his shoulder once more punched it open.

Just then, the bow of the ship was pulled under, and Will was torn out of the cabin. He grabbed the side of the door, holding on against the extreme angle. Just inside was what he was looking for. He saw a cutlass. *Perfect.* Gripping the small pirate's blade, he used the angle of the submerging ship to slide the length of the deck, where he ended in sloshing hurricane waters at the bow. Bracing himself on the rail with one foot and the deck with the other, he grabbed the now-tight rigging and hacked at it with the cutlass. With two hard hacks, the ship was released.

Like a slingshot, Will was tossed yards into the air as the bow popped high above the water. Landing on the deck broke something in his right arm, but he was too pumped up with adrenaline to take note of it. The ship was then consumed by another wave, and he sat still for a moment, collecting his thoughts and energy. The groaning of another ship sounded in the distance, another victim of the sinking rigging. The whole fleet would be wrecked this day.

But not this ship.

With renewed energy as he heard the others ships sink, Will climbed the deck. At the top, the wind was deafening. Barely able to stand, he braced himself on the wheel, which was spinning out of control. He gripped it and briefly wondered what direction he was supposed to go.

Looking through the piercing rain, he searched the seascape. Seeing only mountains of water, he had no ideas. The current was heading in a single direction, and it was good enough to deduce he had to go the opposite direction to the current. Glancing up at the sails didn't give him much encouragement. They had been ripped apart and torn into useless shreds. To test his discouragement, Will tried turning the wheel. The ship didn't change direction.

He stared blankly into the distance, watching the walls of water appear and disappear all around him. The sun was setting now, and the wind was intolerable. The water bruised his face. His clothes were as shredded as the useless sails above him. His arm was frozen into place, and he had dull throbs pounding through his chest. His exhaustion was overwhelming, and he felt like repeating the Barrister's dying words.

A loud creak interrupted his thoughts. Looking back, he saw a towering wall of water. The force of a hundred men smashing him to the deck, sending spikes of lightning through his mind, and then all went dark.

# SEVENTY

It was hot. A gentle slap on the face brought him back from deep in his consciousness. He was parched. Wet. Broken. It was too bright to open his eyes, but another gentle pat on his cheek did bring him further along. Pain bellowed through his head, and a groan fell out of his mouth.

Squinting through the bright light, he saw Dorothy's face leaning over him with worried eyes. The sky was cloudless. The distant creak of a ship sang in his ears. He heard seagulls. Her brown eyes softened at his waking.

"You made it," the words gasped from his mouth and a cough poured out.

"So did you." She smiled.

Mr. Wilkinson stood next to her.

"You've done very well, Sir Shakespeare. You are a tribute to the knighthood."

"And you, sir," he managed to say.

Leaning up on his good arm, Will looked around, surprised at the calm nature of the surrounding sea.

"The hurricane passed?"

"Fortunately for you, it hit the Caribbean. We're far enough away that we just got the edge of it."

"That was the edge?"

"Strongest recorded hurricane to pass through here in years. They clocked her at 260 kilometers per hour at Abaco Island. She's heading straight for Fort Lauderdale. It won't be pretty."

Gripping his head, he looked around again, stunned that he'd survived the night.

"You found me," he whispered, slowly regaining his voice.

"It wasn't hard. Not many medieval ships in Bermuda these days," Wilkinson smiled.

"The Grail?" He asked.

"Down below. You should have a gander."

Dorothy helped him stand. Everything hurt, but it didn't matter. Neither did the monstrous hunger pains in his stomach or his dehydrated throat. Limping over to the hold, he looked inside. Dorothy shone a light.

It was rather anticlimactic. Stacks and stacks of ancient crates met his eye. They were sealed, and even from this angle, he could tell they were airtight. At first glance, there appeared to be hundreds of them.

"The only existing documents from the Library of Alexandria," Wilkinson said.

Will cast confused eyes on the aging man.

"We have a lot to do, Sir William."

Wilkinson was holding the cutlass Will had used to free the ship, and his heart jumped. He couldn't handle another betrayal. Not now. Not another fight. There was nothing else in him. Before he could sink into desperation, he saw that the old man was knighting him.

"As Miss Dorothy Wilkinson is my witness, and with the highest authority in the Poor Fellow-Soldiers of Christ and the Temple of Solomon, I hereby knight thee Master and Commander who's sworn duty is defend the pious, aid and comfort the persecuted, the sick and the poor, to fight the with virtue and charity and to abhor all immodesty and illegitimate pleasures of the flesh. Glory be to the Father, and to the Son, and to the Holy Ghost. Amen."

Will stared, mouth wide open.

"Caretaking the Holy Grail means taking the highest office a knight can have. I've just made you second in command."

"You're the grand master?"

Dorothy was just as stunned.

And then before Will could say anything more, Mr. Wilkinson took his daughter's hand.

"I have been preparing you for this day, Dorothy, although I'd hoped it would be under different circumstances. I wish to invite you into the Order as Dame and take the oath as a Poor Fellow-Soldier."

"Can we take this ship back to the sound, before someone sees her?" She responded.

Mr. Wilkinson smiled, "So we'll discuss it later?"

She put a gentle hand on her father's face and said, "We have a long road ahead of us. Let's just take it one day at a time, shall we?"

Looking back into the darkened hold, a smile at last illuminated Will's face.

# Acknowledgments

I owe a tremendous debt of gratitude to my family, who have persisted with my fictionalized version of reality for all these years. My mother and father--thanks for putting me in writing classes with a bunch of adults when I was 10. That takes a certain amount of parental magic to nurture this quirky side of me.

Thank you to my Mother-In-Law who read a version of this book back when it took place in Berlin. Her appetite for my fiction keeps me writing.

Thank you also to my equally fiction-passionate wife. I know you've heard your fill of Templar stories and conspiracy theories, but without our kitchen chats I'd be lost. Your are my light and eternal guide. I love you.

Thanks to my colleagues and friends at the agency. Noemi, Stefan, and Will, you've given me an incredible treasure chest of skills and insights that have made me grow as a professional and a writer. Your blind support of my double literary life is very much appreciated. Looking forward to years of partnership to come.

Thank you to Sir Michael. You are an inspiration to what a modern knight can and should be. Keep up the movement so that more of us can "rise a knight."

Special thanks to Dr. Lomas who intervened at the last minute and helped me to avoid serious Knight Templar blunders. You are an honor to the craft and I'm thrilled and humbled to have access to your help and insights.